Acknowledgements

My deep gratitude for her shrewd critiquing goes to my fellow writer and friend, Barbara Winter. I'd also like to thank members of the Fiction Highway Guild, whose insightful comments helped me to polish the manuscript.

Thanks to creative writing instructor Brian Henry, whose excellent writing courses and workshops have improved my skills and allowed me to meet other writers. Also, to John Scutt, who gave me valuable information on police interview procedures, and to Kenneth Gansel, who provided lively insights on Port Dover's annual motor bike rally.

Heartfelt thanks to my family and friends for their enthusiastic support, especially to my husband Ted who read countless drafts, gave thoughtful feedback and listened attentively to my ideas about plots and story lines.

> For my husband Ted who loves me when it's easy
> And when it takes all the patience in the world.

In Memory of Peter Rowlands

Dottie Flowers sat in a traffic jam, tapping her fingers on the steering wheel. What a dumb idea to go shoe shopping in rush hour! A sudden jolt from behind made her lurch forward with such force that she broke two freshly manicured fingernails on the dashboard. Damn! She turned around. A plump blonde woman wearing purple-winged sunglasses climbed out of the car behind her. Dottie rolled down the window.

"So sorry," the woman trilled. "No damage done—well, a bit of a scratch on your fender and a small dent." She smiled. "I'm Mabel Scattergood. And you are?"

Dottie gritted her teeth. "We need to exchange insurance information!"

"Are you all right, dear?" Mabel's face grew serious. "You look a bit flushed. Tell you what. Come to my house, and I'll make you a cup of tea. It's the best thing for shock. Remember: 'Every cloud has a silver lining.'"

Dottie couldn't believe her ears. The woman had damaged her car, caused two fingernails to break, and had the nerve to invite her for tea!

"My nephew is trying to sell his motorbike," Mabel explained. "I've allowed him to park it on my driveway until a buyer comes along, but there's plenty of room for your car."

"Do you know what make it is?"

"Make? I haven't a clue."

The invitation provided a perfect opportunity for Dottie to examine the bike. If she liked the look of it, she could make an offer. She muttered her thanks.

A few minutes later, Dottie was ensconced in Mabel's living room. As they sipped Earl Grey tea in the cluttered room, Mabel told Dottie about the challenge of passing her driving test. "These examiners worry too much about trivial things."

"What kind of trivial things?"

"I drove through a school zone at 60."

"The school zone's 40."

"That's not much over the limit!" She'd finally passed after three attempts. "Once I had my driver's license, I signed up for skydiving lessons."

"Skydiving! Are you serious?" Mabel looked to be about Dottie's age. "Oh yes, dear. It's a very invigorating experience. You should try it some time. There's a special rate for seniors." She smiled. "It's never too late to learn, you know."

Dottie admired Mabel's feistiness. A woman after her own heart! She found herself telling Mabel about her move from Montreal more than three years ago, the real estate business she owned, and her cat Muggins. In spite of the inauspicious beginning, Dottie began to like this warmhearted, generous woman. What had started out as a disaster ended on a positive note, even though the motorbike had turned out to be an old wreck with a rusty tailpipe.

It wasn't until she climbed into bed that Dottie realized she'd forgotten to take down the insurance information.

CHAPTER 1

Dottie recognized Henry the moment she spotted him by the hydrangea bushes. The still legs and the awkward angle of the head told her that he was no longer living. Swallowing hard, she placed a hand on his back, just to make sure. It was cold and stiff.

Henry had a nasty temper, and over the years, he'd made plenty of enemies. Maybe this time, he'd met his match. Dottie peered at the inert body. A child's sticker of a skull and crossbones clung to his right ear. *How'd he pick that up*, she wondered. Except for old scars criss-crossing his nose, she couldn't see any fresh injuries. However, she did notice a fish tail protruding from his mouth.

Whatever the cause of Henry's death, she wished it had happened somewhere else. She blew out a long hard breath. How could she tell her neighbour, Gert Bottomley, that her beloved cat was dead, and more to the point, had died on Dottie's lawn?

She spotted Larry, Gert's husband, standing on his veranda, smoking. She'd better get this over with. When she broke the news, sweat broke out on Larry's forehead, and his face grew deathly pale. Dottie, afraid he might pass out, made him sit down. He took a couple of hard drags on his cigarette.

"It's not Henry." Larry's voice was barely audible. "Henry's asleep on our sofa."

"It's not Henry? That's good news," she said. "I wonder who the cat belongs to."

Larry's eyes darted around the veranda. He squished out his cigarette in an ashtray. "It's a stray cat, I expect."

After a few minutes, his colour returned, and he managed a smile. "I'm okay now, Dottie. You run along. And don't worry about the cat. I'll get rid of it."

Later, as Dottie ate breakfast, she spotted Larry through the kitchen window, lifting the body into a plastic bag. *What had made him so afraid?* she wondered.

CHAPTER 2

Making the most of a rare day off, Dottie Flowers was on her third cup of black coffee when the mail arrived. She stretched her arms and yawned. This is what retirement would be like—lazy breakfasts with the paper spread out over the table. But what would she do once she'd finished reading the news and the obituaries? Forget about retiring, she told herself. It was too depressing.

As she folded up the paper, a headline caught her attention: "Dead Cats Found in Sandy Lane: Were they Poisoned?" Dottie felt the blood drain from her face. Sandy Lane was only six blocks away. It brought back unpleasant memories of the cat she'd found in her garden two days ago.

Dottie's eyes darted around the living room. She breathed a sigh of relief when she saw Muggins's orange tail dangling over the edge of the sofa. Dottie made up her mind. From now on, he wouldn't be allowed out on his own. He wouldn't like that one little bit.

She checked the mailbox just outside her front door and found the usual assortment of junk mail and bills. One flyer, in bright blue lettering with pictures of dice scattered over the yellow paper, announced a seniors' trip to Casino Rama. An image popped into her head of a busload of elderly folk tottering into the casino to sit at slot machines for hours on end. As she scrunched the paper into a ball, Larry's wife, Gert, appeared. Tall and skinny, with tightly permed grey hair, Gert peered at Dottie over half-moon glasses. She handed Dottie a letter. "This is for you. That mailman always mixes up the mail." As Gert turned to leave, she stared through Dottie's living room window. "I'm glad that vicious cat of yours is in the house. It's just as well you keep him there, so he can't attack my Henry."

The relationship between the two women had started on the wrong foot the day Dottie moved into her bungalow. Henry and Muggins got into a fierce battle, and Muggins limped home with a bloodied nose and a piece of his ear missing. Right behind him marched Gert, holding a struggling black cat. Blood oozed from the tip of the cat's tail, and clumps of fur stuck up in all directions. Her face pink with fury, Gert had proclaimed, "Look what your beast did to my Henry!"

As weeks went by, the complaints grew. Once, as Dottie arrived home from work, Gert confronted her. "Ever since you moved in, me and my Larry haven't had a moment's peace," she seethed, her voice full of venom. "Your cat always uses my strawberry patch to do his business. And the exhaust of that fancy car of yours spews poisonous fumes all over my flowerbeds!"

Dottie shuddered as she recalled the incident and hurried indoors. She wondered how the good-natured Larry ended up married to such an overbearing woman. Apart from constantly complaining, something about Gert gave her the creeps.

She glanced at the mail. At the top of the pile lay an envelope with the words "Are you looking for a life partner? Soul Mates Inc. can help. Just fill out the enclosed questionnaire. No obligation to join." Another piece of junk for the garbage. There had to be an easier way to meet men.

She had a sudden image of Fred Fortune in scruffy jeans, his grey hair tied back in a ponytail. Fred, whom she'd last seen naked thirty-five years ago at Woodstock, had landed on her doorstep four days ago, and in a moment of weakness, she'd agreed to have dinner with him next week. What could she have been thinking? She must phone him and cancel the date. Now, all she needed was a good excuse.

10

Her eyes grazed over the white envelope with gold letters lying on the hall table. It contained an invitation to a charity dinner to be held the same night as her date with Fred Fortune. Relieved to have a valid reason for turning him down, she punched in his phone number. As she rehearsed what to say, a voice announced that the number was no longer in service. Had she misdialled? She tried again, but the same thing happened. "Blast!" she muttered. "I bet it's been cut off because he hasn't paid the phone bill. So now, I'm stuck with Fred, like it or not." She lit one of her cigarillos and took a deep drag. They'd have dinner. She'd tell him she had a very early real estate meeting, so she couldn't stay up late, and that would be the end of it.

As she smoked, she caught her reflection in the mirror above the hall table and examined her face. Her dark, almond-shaped eyes helped to soften a sharp nose and protruding chin, although small wrinkles—crow's feet, her friend Mabel called them—had developed in the corners. Her shoulder-length hair, worn in a bun at work, had a rich auburn gleam, thanks to regular visits to the hairdresser. Tall, willowy, with a weakness for designer clothes, and elegant shoes, Dottie worked out three times a week at the local "Y." She managed to keep her figure slim and well-toned, except for flabby upper arms and the "spare tire" around her waist that no amount of exercise would budge. Yet, the flabby arms and spare tire paled in comparison to the recent discovery of spider veins on her legs.

Dottie was about to toss the mail on the table to sift through later, when a pink envelope caught her eye. She sniffed at the envelope. Perfumed stationery! Alarm bells went off when she recognized Mabel's copperplate handwriting. Yesterday, they'd had words on the phone. "I'm not going white water rafting, Mabel."

"The company has an excellent safety record," Mabel had assured her. "They haven't had a drowning since 2005."

"2005! That's only a year ago! You seem to forget I can't swim."

"You don't have to swim. You'll be on an inflated raft wearing a life jacket."

"I'm terrified of water. After four sets of lessons, I decided that swimming isn't for me."

"You'll have so much fun you'll forget your fear."

"No! And that's my final word on the subject!"

Dottie put on her rhinestone-framed glasses and gingerly removed a brochure from the envelope. "Warrendale Spa offers you the benefit of beautifying, balancing, calming, detoxifying, and revitalizing your body and soul." Interesting! She read on. "We offer Swedish massage, herbal body wraps, moor mud treatments…" Mud treatments?

Though she rather fancied going to the spa, mud treatments held no appeal since that awful experience on the Trepanier winery ride last Sunday when her horse shied, and she was catapulted into a muddy ditch. Even worse, she'd landed on top of George Fernandes, a creep from high school days. Her white safari shirt and beige cotton slacks had been splattered with slimy mud, her new Mephistos ruined.

Dottie turned over the spa brochure and found a yellow Post-It note stuck on the back. "My niece Yolanda is a regular client. She swears by them. They have an all-inclusive weekend package deal on right now. I'll give you a call tonight. Mabel." Dottie might have guessed Mabel's domineering niece was behind this. Placing the brochure on one side, she cleared away the breakfast dishes. It was just another of Mabel's nutty ideas! This past week, she'd been obsessed with white-water rafting; next week, it could be paragliding.

Thinking about the winery ride reminded her of an article in yesterday's newspaper about a robbery in Trepanier's vineyard. Twelve dozen cases of wine had been stolen. Did this have anything to do with George Fernandes? Dottie recalled George had stolen lunch money and cheated on tests in high school. It would explain why he and those sleazy-looking friends of his, Billy and Den, took the trail ride. Using the ride as a cover-up, maybe they had been "casing the joint," just as Mabel had speculated.

Mabel had also suggested they might be members of the Skinner gang. When Dottie questioned her, Mabel confessed that she'd gleaned the information about the ruthless gang from Karla Jackman. Karla, a member of Mabel's bridge club, tended to embellish her stories to impress friends.

Dottie found her leather gardening gloves and trowel. After a rainstorm during the night, the sun shone in a clear blue sky, a perfect day for outside work. Muggins settled under a rosebush at the foot of the garden, watching her through half-closed eyes. For the next two hours, she immersed herself in weeding, digging, and pruning. As she dug around the hydrangea bushes, her eyes fell on the patch of flat grass where the poor cat had lain. She shuddered, thankful that Larry had removed the body.

A car door slammed, and within seconds, a loud voice called out, "Cooee! Anyone home?" Around the corner sailed Mabel, wearing a bright floral shirt and hot-pink Bermuda shorts. "There you are. You'll have a stroke working in this heat!" She handed Dottie a plastic shopping bag. "I've brought you some old *Hello* magazines. Yolanda dropped them off yesterday, and I know you enjoy reading them." Overcome with a sudden attack of sneezing, Mabel rooted in her shorts pocket for a tissue.

Dottie felt a rush of affection for her friend's thoughtfulness. "Thanks, Mabel. I'm just about to get myself a glass of lemonade. Would you like one?"

"How very civilized! Thank you, dear," Mabel said, dabbing her nose. "My allergies are acting up. Would you mind if we have our drinks indoors?"

There goes my peaceful day off, thought Dottie. Still, she'd managed to get in a couple of hours' gardening. "That's a good idea. It's cool inside as well." As the back door squeaked open, Muggins trotted across the lawn and followed her indoors.

Dottie set out glasses and a pitcher of lemonade on the kitchen table. Occupied with making sure the napkins were folded properly and the mats straight, she only half listened to Mabel's gabbling.

"So, what do you think? We can leave first thing Saturday morning."

"Sorry, Mabel, what did you say?"

"I suggest we stop at Casino Rama on the way to the spa. A flyer in the mail gave me the idea."

"Oh, that. I got one too. Forget it. As far as I'm concerned, gambling's a total waste of money. And you seem to forget I'm a working woman with a real estate business."

"Surely, you can take a weekend off occasionally. All work and no play makes Jack a dull boy. Anyway, I thought you'd cut back your hours."

"I've cut down on the number of clients I take on, and I do take the occasional day off like today, but in the real estate business, you've got to be flexible. Weekends are often our busiest times."

"The special only lasts until the end of the month, and I've booked us for next weekend." Mabel sipped her lemonade. "Before you say anything, Dottie, this is on me. Think of it as my way of apologizing for the winery fiasco. It was my idea to take you on a trail ride, but it didn't turn out well, did it?"

"That's an understatement." Remembering why Mabel had taken her on the "Magical Mystery Tour," Dottie felt a surge of guilt. "I know you meant well. You wanted me out of the way so that my family could surprise me with a birthday party." A lump came into her throat as she recalled the event.

They'd driven home from the winery ride in silence. As they'd turned into Dottie's driveway, she saw the balloons, bunches of them, tied on the porch railings. A large brightly coloured banner, *Happy 60th. Birthday, Grandma!*, hung crookedly across the porch. Her daughter, Hettie, and son, Jeremy, stood on the porch with their spouses, waving. Bill and Heather, Jeremy's children, had leapt up and down with excitement. "Hurry up, Grandma! We're hungry!"

Dottie looked at Mabel. "So, the spa reservations are for next weekend." She recalled the words from the brochure. "Warrendale incorporates a European approach which favours pampering and nurturing." "I could do with a break," she said, "but I'll have to see if my neighbour Margaret can take care of Muggins. I won't trust him with anyone else, not with a cat killer around."

"Don't be long-winded about it. I have to confirm the booking by tomorrow."

***

It rained most of the way to the casino, and Mabel's windshield wipers squeaked. By the time they reached Orillia, Dottie's head throbbed. She massaged her temples.

"Got a headache, Dottie?"

"You better believe it."

"You need to relax. Gambling will help you to unwind a bit, and the casino's only a few minutes away."

"Anything to get away from that noise!"

"What noise?"

"I can't believe you haven't heard those wiper blades."

"Oh, that," Mabel said. "I've got used to it."

"You might have, but the squeak's driving me mad. It's time you got new ones." Dottie sighed. It was time Mabel got a new car, never mind new wiper blades.

***

Passing by the security personnel, Dottie and Mabel entered the casino. Dottie's head pounded from discordant sounds and the steady hum of machines in the gambling area. The bright lights and row upon row of machines reminded her of pictures she'd seen of Las Vegas. People's eyes were glued to the screens in front of them. No one smiled. "What do I do now?" she whispered to Mabel.

"It's easy." Mabel fed a 20-dollar bill into a machine. "Just make sure the bill is face up." The tokens jingled as they fell into place. "Now, press the Cash Out button. That way, you can play one, two, or three tokens at a time."

"What do you recommend?"

"Well..." Mabel looked at Dottie. "If you go for one at a time, it takes longer to play. On the other hand, if you play three, you could win the jackpot. I'll see you in one hour by the entrance. Good luck!"

"Where are you going?"

"I'm off to play blackjack."

Mabel marched away. Dottie almost called after her but changed her mind. Once she'd lost her 20 dollars, she'd buy a coffee, wait for Mabel, and people-watch. Starting now. Glancing around, she noticed one player, her grey hair in tight curls, busily feeding the machine 20-dollar bills. A bill fluttered to the ground, and as the woman bent to pick it up, Dottie recognized her neighbour, Gert Bottomley. Gert a gambler? She looked around for Larry. He wasn't sitting at any of the nearby machines. Maybe Gert had come by

16

herself or with a friend. Dottie turned her attention to the machine, hoping Gert hadn't seen her.

With the large number of patrons in the casino, the air felt stifling. Dottie removed her jacket and hung it on the back of the chair. She started to play with one token at a time. Five minutes later, she had doubled her money. Feeling braver, she decided to play three at a time. Within minutes, she tripled her original twenty. Tension had melted from her shoulders, and her headache had almost gone. She glanced around the room. Had anyone noticed her good luck? Of course not. They were all too busy.

Within the space of four minutes, her luck changed. Down to her last three tokens, she almost jumped out of her skin when she heard a familiar but unwelcome voice.

"Not having much luck today, Dottie?"

She spun around and stared into the pudgy face of George Fernandes. Behind him lurked Billy and Den, his friends from the winery ride. "What are **you** doing here!"

"Same as you. Only, I play to win." As he pushed his face close to hers, his breath reeked of whisky. "Let me buy you a drink," he slurred. "I'll turn your luck around."

"Go away!"

"Not even one little drink?"

"Get lost, George!" She pushed the button.

The light above her machine flashed, and an alarm went off. What had she done? When people turned to look at her, she felt her face grow warm. Some of them crowded around her, obviously enjoying her embarrassment.

Mabel rushed over, much to Dottie's relief. "I think I broke the machine," said Dottie.

"Oh, no, dear! You've just won a $1,000 jackpot!"

"It must be beginner's luck." Something tugged at her jacket. As she turned, George crumpled to the floor. The shock of seeing her win the jackpot must have been too much for him.

Then, she saw the knife stuck in his back.

CHAPTER 3

D ottie strode out the casino with Mabel trotting at her heels and exclaimed, "I can't believe how long it took the police to question us. You'd think we'd killed poor George!"

"It's 'poor George' now, is it?"

"Let's get out of here!"

"There's a good Italian restaurant quite close to the spa where we can grab a bite of lunch," Mabel said. "We aren't due to arrive until three, so there's plenty of time."

***

As they stepped into the foyer of *La Trattoria*, Al Martino's "Come Share the Wine" played softly in the background. A silver-haired man, formally dressed in a black tuxedo, greeted them. He smiled broadly at Mabel. "Signora Scattergood! How nice to see you again. Please, follow me."

He ushered them to a table overlooking a small herb garden. Both women ordered the pasta special with a glass of Chardonnay. Within minutes, the server brought a basket of bread with olive oil and balsamic vinegar and two glasses of wine.

"So, what do you think of the restaurant?" Mabel asked.

"I'm impressed. How did you know about this place?"

"Yolanda. She found out about it through an article in a magazine. We go to the casino and treat ourselves to lunch here afterwards." Breaking off a piece of bread, Mabel dipped it in olive oil. "Speaking of Yolanda, she was telling me about this con artist in BC. A friend of hers who lives in Victoria knows a woman whom this chap conned. He was very charming, evidently—blond, blue-eyed—looked like Brad somebody or other."

"Pitt."

"What?"

"Brad Pitt," Dottie repeated. "Film star."

"You really know who these celebrities are, Dottie. I should follow your lead and start going to the movies every week."

Their lunches arrived, and the server grated parmesan cheese over the pasta dish. After she left, Mabel closed her eyes and breathed in the aroma of the creamy garlic sauce. "Mm! Smells heavenly!" She picked up her fork and began to eat. "Anyway, it seems this woman owned a couple of paintings which had been left to her by an aunt."

"What woman?"

"The one Yolanda told me about who lives in Victoria...."

Dottie cut in. "Oh, yes. Sorry. Go on."

"She knew the pictures were valuable, but didn't know how much they were worth. This fellow claimed he had a colleague who was art expert, so he persuaded the woman to have them appraised. She gave him the paintings, and that was the last she saw of him."

"She sounds too gullible," Dottie said between mouthfuls of pasta. "I mean, would you give valuable paintings to someone you hardly knew?"

"Of course not."

Two bikers appeared in the doorway of the restaurant, helmets under their arms. They followed the maitre d' to a corner table and sat down. Dottie put down her fork and leaned across the table. "Don't look now," she whispered, "but I think we're being followed."

Mabel's eyes shot wide open. "By whom?"

"Those guys sitting in the corner."

Mabel stole a glance at the two men. "Don't be silly. Really, Dottie, your nerves are in worse shape than mine."

"Remember the trail ride and the rough-looking characters with George Fernandes?" Dottie asked. "That's them. I made a mental note of their names when we all had to introduce ourselves. Den's the bald overweight guy, and Billy's the skinny one."

When Mabel took a longer look, her face paled. "Oh, goodness, you're right. But I think you're overreacting, Dottie. Just because they happen to come into the same restaurant doesn't mean they're following us."

"I have a feeling they are. I don't see them choosing a fancy restaurant like this for lunch."

"Surely, they don't think we killed George!"

"Of course not. But maybe **they** did!" She paused. "The thing is, Billy and Den were with George at the casino, but they weren't around when the police arrived. It's a bit suspicious; don't you think?"

"It does seem odd. Still, why would they follow us? If one of them is the murderer, he'd make himself scarce."

"Let's finish lunch and see what happens."

"I'm ordering ice cream for dessert," Mabel said. "What about you?"

"How can you even think of eating dessert with those thugs just a few yards away?"

"Rushing off might look too obvious."

"We aren't rushing away," Dottie said. "Once we've finished the pasta, we'll ask for the cheque."

They walked out the restaurant into bright sunshine. As they approached the car park, the sun's rays caught the shiny chrome of a Harley Davidson motorbike. "Just look at that! It must belong to Billy and Den." Dottie almost drooled as she gazed upon the huge machine. "This Harley is far too good for creeps like those two."

Dottie's passion for bikes had started back in 1969 at Woodstock when her newfound love, Fred, had taken her for a ride on his Honda. She almost bought a bike once, just before her ex-husband Roger Wilmott had been charged with embezzlement and sent to prison. By the time he'd finished his sentence, all her savings were gone. She'd leased bikes over the years. Now, as retirement grew closer, the longing for her own bike had returned.

"Dottie, hurry up!" Mabel urged. "There they are!"

Dottie glanced around to see Billy and Den standing in front of the restaurant, shading their eyes. After another wistful glance at the bike, Dottie followed Mabel to the car and climbed in. She saw the men walking towards the bike. "Let's go! If they're following us, we'll need a head start."

Mabel put her foot down hard, and the little car spun its wheels, making deep tire marks in the gravel. She screeched out of the car park, right in front of a large trailer. "That's a stroke of luck!"

"Shoot, Mabel, what are you doing!"

Mabel changed gears and accelerated. "Den and Billy won't be able to overtake the trailer on this narrow road. With a bit of luck, we'll lose them!"

Dottie began to think Mabel was right, until a few minutes later, she heard a loud roar. She swung around. "That trailer must have turned down a side road. The Harley's weaving in and out of traffic, and it's getting close."

"Did you bring your cell phone?"

"I always carry it with me. Why?"

"We'd better call the police."

Dottie looked at her friend in surprise. "Whatever for?"

"They're obviously following, and they might be armed and dangerous. What if they're members of the Skinner gang I told you about?" Mabel caught Dottie's eye. "All right, I know Karla Jackman exaggerates. Still, they could be gangsters."

"You read too many thrillers."

Mabel's face lit up. "I have an idea."

Dottie's antennae went on full alert. "What kind of idea?"

"Just watch!"

For more than an hour, Mabel drove the car up and down winding country roads, making Dottie's head spin. At one point, she took a sudden turn down a dirt track. A farm dog ran towards the car, barking ferociously, and Mabel just had time to close her window before it leapt up, barring its teeth and growling. A florid-faced man in dungarees marched over and told them, in very colourful language, to get off his land.

They hoped Den and Billy had lost their trail. No such luck. As soon as they got back on the road, they heard the familiar roar a short distance away. They finally got a break. They'd just passed another farm when Dottie glanced back and noticed that a tractor pulling a flat truck filled with hay bales had edged out of the farm lane onto the road, blocking all traffic.

A few minutes later, she and Mabel reached the main road and saw a sign in gold lettering for Warrendale Spa. They turned down a lane, and around a bend, a farm with horse barns came into view. Mabel slowed down as a couple of young riders on horseback trotted past. Beyond the farm lay the spa, a large Victorian house set in beautifully manicured grounds.

Mabel mopped her brow with a tissue. "Thank goodness, we're finally here!" She glanced around. "There's no sign of the bike. I think we've lost them."

While Mabel parked the car, Dottie rang the bell. A young woman wearing a crisp peach-coloured uniform opened the door. In a husky voice, she welcomed Dottie to Warrendale. "My name is Miranda. I'll be taking care of you during your stay."

Once Mabel joined them, Miranda ushered them into the hallway, its sand-coloured walls an attractive complement to the terra-cotta tiled floor where ferns sat in oversized clay pots. Lush green plants hung from the ceiling.

They followed Miranda up a short flight of steps to their suite. The wicker furniture and pine floor created a warm atmosphere, ideal for a relaxing weekend.

Miranda did a quick check of the bedrooms and bathroom. "Everything seems to be in order," she said. "If you need anything, please call the front desk. Dinner is served between six and eight. The dinner menu is over there with our breakfast and lunch menus." She pointed to a round table by the window. "The food here is excellent," she added with a bright smile. "Our chef is renowned throughout North America."

Once Miranda left, they sank into comfortable armchairs. "I hope we've seen the last of Billy and Den," Mabel said. "I wish we knew why they're following us."

"Let's try to forget about it for now." Dottie perused the menu. "Miranda's right. The food sounds good. I must admit, I'm feeling hungry after all that excitement."

"Me too. I think I'll have a quick shower before dinner."

"Go ahead. Do you want a whisky?" She knew Mabel enjoyed the occasional Scotch.

"You brought Scotch? Good planning! Not too strong, though. What about ice?"

Dottie took a quick look in the freezer compartment of the mini fridge. "No problem. The trays are full."

After preparing the drinks, Dottie retrieved a packet of cheese biscuits from her suitcase. The biscuits would stave off hunger pangs for a while. She wandered over to the French doors and saw, with pleasure, that the room had a small balcony. "Perfect!" she thought. "I can smoke without disturbing Mabel."

Rummaging for cigarillos and lighter, she felt something bulky in the jacket pocket. She drew out a brown envelope, creased and grubby, as though it had been pushed into a small space and left there for a long time. Slitting the envelope open, she peered inside. She dashed to the bathroom door. "Mabel! Come here, quick!"

Mabel emerged from the bathroom, swathed in a white towelling robe. "What on earth's the matter?"

"I know why Billy and Den are following us. Look at this!"

She spread the contents of the envelope on the dresser. A matching set of diamond and emerald jewelry, consisting of a necklace, earrings, and ring, sparkled in the lamplight. "I found these in my jacket."

"Oh, my!" Mabel stared at the magnificent jewelry. "Look at the size of the diamond in the ring! It's so big it almost looks artificial. And those emeralds!"

"I don't know much about jewelry, but I can recognize valuable gems when I see them. These pieces must be worth a fortune."

"How did they get into your jacket?"

"George must have put them there."

"George is dead, in case you've forgotten!"

"Just before he was murdered, he came over to my slot machine and started talking to me," Dottie said. "I tried to put him off, but he muttered something about buying me a drink. When the lights started to flash, he must have stuck the envelope into the pocket. I haven't a clue why."

"Because he knew someone was following him. Why else would he put it there?"

Dottie closed her eyes and tried to remember the events leading to George's stabbing. She'd hung her jacket on the back of the chair and remembered feeling a tug just before George had been murdered. Had George planted the envelope in her jacket for safety, intending to retrieve it later?

"Did you tell the police that you spoke with George?"

"No. If they hadn't kept going over the same ground, I might have said something. I got tired of being pestered."

"You have withheld what might be vital information, Dottie Flowers! You could be in really hot water over this."

Dottie's antipathy towards the police stemmed from a bad experience when she had been accused, with her ex-husband, of embezzlement. She'd never told anyone about Roger, not even her close friend Mabel, and preferred to keep it that way.

She thought about Billy and Den suddenly disappearing from the casino. Maybe they saw someone stab George and panicked. Dottie gulped down a large mouthful of Scotch. She hoped that was why they left. The alternative didn't bear thinking about.

Glancing at the dinner menu lying on the bed, Mabel frowned. "I can't even think about food now."

"Neither can I." Dottie finished her drink. "Let's make it an early night. We'll feel much better with a good night's sleep." She returned the jewelry to the envelope. "I'll go down to the front desk right away and put the jewelry in the safe."

"Good thinking. In the meantime, I'm going to put some of that replenishing cream I bought in the dollar shop on my face. My skin is bound to suffer with all this stress."

After securing the jewelry in the hotel safe, Dottie wandered onto the balcony and lit a cigarillo. Daylight had begun to fade, and the air had cooled off a bit. Closing her eyes, she leaned on the balcony and took a long drag. The tension in her shoulders faded away. *It's peaceful here*, she thought, *a perfect place to unwind and relax.*

In the garden below, flowering shrubs swayed gently and rustled in the light breeze. As she smoked, Dottie saw a movement in the shrubs. Probably a deer searching for food. She kept her eyes glued on the same spot. Suddenly, a face peeked through a gap in the foliage, and then disappeared. Heart pounding, she stepped back inside the French doors. She shook herself. It had been a long stressful day, and maybe her imagination was playing tricks.

She went inside and locked the French doors, just in case.

CHAPTER 4

The fading light cast its shadow over the small sitting room. Dottie settled on the sofa, the spa booklet on her lap. She couldn't get the image of the ghostly face out of her mind. Looking for a distraction, she flicked through the booklet and found an article on mud baths. "Visitors who have never taken a mud bath are naturally curious about the treatment," she read. "Apprehensive, more like it!" she muttered.

"What did you say, Dottie?" Mabel yelled from the bathroom.

"I'm reading about mud baths!"

Mabel stuck her head around the door, her face covered in thick white cream. "Marvellous things!" she enthused. "My niece Yolanda swears by them. We could try one tomorrow."

"Maybe."

Dottie read on. "At Warrendale Spa, couples can enjoy a bath together. The treatment begins when you slip into a tub of fine clay-based mud. You can feel yourself relax as the mud treatment detoxifies, soothes aching muscles, and leaves you refreshed and renewed." In the picture, a man and woman lay in mud up to their chins, smiling at each other. *I can think of more interesting things to do with my husband than lie in a mud bath*, Dottie thought. *I wonder how much they were paid to do that.*

***

The next morning, Dottie awoke to dazzling sunlight pouring through half-opened blinds. Hunger pains gripped her stomach. What with the stress of being followed and the discovery of the emerald jewelry, all she'd consumed since lunchtime yesterday was a Scotch. Observing the empty packet of cheese biscuits, Dottie smiled. At least they didn't go to waste! If there were any food around, Mabel would find it.

Putting on her glasses, she scanned the breakfast menu, which looked very healthy. But where was the coffee? The thought of foregoing her morning caffeine fix didn't please her. Mabel would have to drive her to the nearest coffee shop. Speaking of her friend, where had she gone?

A key turned in the lock. "Are you up yet?" Mabel called out.

"Not yet. Come into my bedroom."

Dressed in a canary yellow sundress and wearing a wide-brimmed straw hat, Mabel waltzed in. "It's a glorious day! Do hurry up and get ready! Our pedicures are booked for 10. We've just got time for a quick breakfast." She glanced over the menu that Dottie handed her. "Sounds healthy! Don't be too long. I'm ravenous."

"You go ahead. I'll meet you by the pool in 10 minutes."

Dottie showered quickly and slipped into white linen slacks, gold sandals, and a navy silk top. Maybe muesli and herbal tea would do the trick, but she doubted it.

***

Patio tables with coral pink umbrellas and matching cushioned chairs were set around a large kidney-shaped pool. Women occupied many of the tables. Men have more sense than to waste time in a spa, Dottie decided. The food, laid out on a long table, looked delicious. Dottie filled her plate with yoghurt, fresh fruit, and juice and joined Mabel at one of the patio tables.

Mabel sipped a cup of herbal tea. On the table in front of her sat a half-eaten muffin. "Sorry, I should have waited for you."

Dottie dismissed Mabel's apology with a flick of her hand. "Don't worry about it." After a few mouthfuls of yoghurt, she sighed with pleasure. "That's better!"

Mabel's eyes swept over the guests around her, and then back at Dottie. "I think I saw Den about five minutes ago."

"What!" Dottie's spoon clattered onto the deck. "Are you sure it was Den?"

"Well, someone who looked a lot like him. He was hovering near the rose garden." She took a bite of muffin. "Of course, many men are bald."

"I thought I saw someone in the garden last night." Dottie explained what happened. "If you're right, it was probably him or Billy looking through the bushes. I bet they were waiting for us to go for dinner, so they could search for the jewelry."

"They might be breaking into our suite at this very moment!"

Dottie munched on a fat strawberry. "I'm glad the jewelry's in the hotel safe."

Mabel lowered her voice. "We need to look in the rose garden."

"Are you crazy? We know Den and Billy are after the jewelry. That's why they've been following us. They might have murdered George Fernandes. I don't plan to spend my spare time tracking down murderers in the rose garden!"

"But we must be on the alert."

"Mabel! I'm not going to search for Den and Billy. Neither are you. Besides, you're allergic to pollen; you could have a sneezing fit."

"Good point. What we should be doing is phoning the police."

"What would you say to them?" Dottie countered. "We think we've seen one of the men who followed us yesterday, and we think he might have killed George Fernandes? Let's keep the police out of it for now."

"I get the impression that you have a thing about the police."

"How do you mean?"

"Each time I've suggested getting the police involved, you back off."

Dottie blew out a long breath. "You're right. It's time I filled you in." She told Mabel about her marriage to Roger Wilmott. "When Roger was accused of embezzlement, the police were sure I was his accomplice. They questioned me for hours before they finally let me go."

"No wonder it's left a bad taste in your mouth."

"It's more like a phobia. I still get nightmares about the interrogation." She forced herself to smile. "Let's get on to more cheerful things."

"Like pedicures."

Dottie finished the yoghurt. "I'd like you to do me a favour. Drive me to the nearest coffee shop as soon as we have some free time. I desperately need some coffee."

Mabel glanced at her watch. "It'll have to be after the pedicures because we've only got another 15 minutes before our appointments. I'm going to have another of those delicious blueberry muffins. Would you like one?"

Dottie shook her head. "No, thanks, I have plenty here."

***

The soft music and the gentle voices of the attendants soothed Dottie's spirits. "I don't have a craving for caffeine any more," she told Mabel after they'd had their pedicures. "Whoever would believe that a foot massage could do that?"

"The Chinese are big believers in foot massages," Mabel said. "Did you know foot massage places are set up on almost every corner in Beijing? They're as common as coffee shops are in Canada."

I bet Mabel gleaned that information from know-it-all Yolanda, Dottie thought unkindly.

In the next two hours, they received hand massages and a paraffin wax treatment. The pampering started to grow on Dottie, and she looked forward to the afternoon. Maybe even the mud bath might turn out to be enjoyable.

***

They were ushered into a small room dimly lit with candles. After undressing, they placed their clothes on a wooden bench and pulled on bathing suits. Dottie walked to the edge of the bath and slowly immersed herself in the warm mud. As the deep heat penetrated her body, she glanced at Mabel in the tub next to her. "This is very relaxing. I can't believe that mud would feel this good!"

Mabel smiled. "We'll have a hot mineral Jacuzzi next. Then, we'll be wrapped in a warm blanket in a darkened room to rest and cool down. This is the life!"

Dottie leaned back on the soft air pillow. The tension began to melt away from her shoulders. She closed her eyes and, within minutes, dozed off.

A creaking noise woke her up. Glancing towards the door, she saw a large bald-headed man looming in the doorway. "It's Den!" Dottie yelled as she struggled out of the bath.

Den strode towards the bench where their clothes lay, but in his haste, he tripped on the edge of the bathtub. "Fuck!" he cursed and toppled headlong into the black goo. He landed with such force that mud flew everywhere.

"Hurry up, Dottie!" Mabel shouted as they ran towards the door to the Jacuzzi room. Heart pounding, Dottie didn't notice the puddle of water near the door until it was too late. Her feet, already slathered in mud, slipped on the wet floor. As she fell, Dottie saw Den, covered in mud, heading towards her.

***

Propped up by pillows, Dottie held the ice bag to her head. The bedroom door opened, and Mabel struggled in with a large tray. "I cajoled the kitchen staff into letting me bring you some food."

"How did you manage that?"

"I told them you have a headache, which is true, but I wasn't about to tell them why."

"It's just about gone." The aroma of vegetable soup made Dottie's mouth water. She checked her watch. "It's already 6 o'clock! No wonder I'm hungry. Have you eaten, or did you bring enough for two?"

Mabel placed the tray on the bed beside Dottie and pulled up a chair. "I ate, but I brought extra just in case. The soup's delicious, and there's brie cheese and a spinach salad."

Dottie took several mouthfuls of soup and ate a slice of brie. "That feels great. Thanks, Mabel." An image of Den, mud dripping from his arms and legs, sprang into her head, and she started to chuckle.

"What's the joke?"

"It's hard to believe that someone who looked like the creature from the black lagoon is trying to harm us."

"He's going to have a hard time chasing us from now on."

"Oh?"

"Den must have panicked when he saw you sprawled out on the floor. He escaped through the emergency exit door that opens onto the garden and tried to hide in the bushes. Someone spotted him. People started to scream, and a couple of the guests chased him. It looks like he broke his leg when he tripped over a garden chair."

"Where is he now?"

"At the local hospital."

"That still leaves Billy." Dottie shuddered at the thought. Somehow, Den didn't seem as spooky as the scar-faced Billy.

"It gives me the creeps when I think that someone—probably Billy—was in here looking for the jewelry while we were in the mud bath."

"How long did it take you to tidy up the room after it was ransacked?"

"A good hour. Still, no damage was done." Mabel popped a cherry tomato into her mouth. "Why do you suppose Den came into the mud bath room?"

"Probably checking to see if we'd taken the emeralds with us. He was heading towards that bench where we left our clothes when he fell into the tub."

"There's nothing we can do tonight," Mabel pointed out. "As Doris Day said, 'tomorrow is another day.'"

"It was Vivien Leigh in *Gone with the Wind.*"

"Whatever. You're the film buff." She looked critically at the food on the tray. "All you've had so far is the soup and a piece of cheese. There's salad and a fruit concoction of some kind."

Dottie helped herself to salad. "How long was I unconscious?"

"At a guess, I'd say probably no more than 30 seconds."

"I remember trying to get the mud off with those white towels."

"They were supposed to be used to dry ourselves after the Jacuzzi," Mabel said, helping herself to some fruit. "I'll never forget the look of horror on the attendant's face when she saw what we were doing. Even when I explained you weren't feeling well and needed to get back to our suite as quickly as possible, she was unsympathetic."

"You can't blame her for being annoyed."

"No, of course not, we were supposed to soak ourselves for 15 minutes in the Jacuzzi first. Thank goodness Miranda appeared. She took charge, and we two helped you back to the room."

"I remember. Sort of."

She patted Dottie's hand. "Never mind—you're safe; that's the main thing."

Dottie blew out a long breath. "For now."

***

The following morning, the police questioned some of the guests, including Dottie and Mabel. One woman, her face red with excitement, came up to them as they ate a late breakfast by the pool. "Have you heard about the intruder? My friend overheard someone say that he's an actor. They're filming a horror movie nearby."

As soon as the woman left, Mabel laughed. "A man told me he'd heard it on good authority that it was a publicity drive for the spa! Can you imagine anyone believing such rubbish!" Mabel helped herself to another muffin. "This is low in fat," she remarked, cutting it in half and slathering a thick layer of butter on each piece.

"What's the point of eating a low-fat muffin when you put all that butter on it!"

Mabel's face grew pink. "We're on holiday. I'll go back to my diet when we get home."

Dottie had suggested recently that cutting out snacks would help, and Mabel had taken umbrage. "I don't snack," she'd countered. "I might have the odd Boston cream donut now and then, but dairy products are good for my bones."

By noon, the guests were once again indulging in full-body hot stone massages, aromatic facemasks, and raindrop therapy. Even the mud bath had been cleaned up and reopened for business. Dottie and Mabel spent a relaxing few hours receiving the massages and herbal facials that they'd missed the previous day.

Around four, Dottie retrieved the emeralds from the hotel safe and stood in line to check out. As she waited, a suitcase wobbled over, and the man in front of Dottie stepped back to avoid it. The heel of his shoe crunched her big toe.

"Ouch!" cried Dottie, wincing with pain.

The man turned around. *Wow—where did he come from,* Dottie wondered as she caught a glimpse of deep brown eyes and dark wavy hair.

"I'm very sorry." He spoke in a soft voice. When he looked at her sandaled feet, his brow furrowed. "That must have been very painful."

"I'll be fine. Nothing's broken."

***

"It's been an interesting experience," Dottie remarked as they got into the car. An image of the handsome stranger flashed into her head. "In more ways than one."

Mabel agreed. "There's been no sign of Billy. Let's hope that's the last we see of the two of them."

As they were about to drive away, Dottie noticed a Jaguar pulling out of the car park ahead of them. She recognised the driver as the man who'd stepped on her foot. A blonde woman in sunglasses sat in the passenger seat beside him, busily filing her nails. Dottie sighed. It seemed all the eligible men were either married or involved with someone.

Blue sky and bright sunshine matched their cheerful mood as they took the old Highway 2 route home. For once, Mabel kept to the speed limit. "I can't remember the last time I drove this slowly," she said. "I do hope that Fifi has been behaving herself at the kennels."

"I'm lucky I've got my neighbour Margaret to look after Muggins. It's taken a while, but now he's used to her and allows her to pick him up. He even curls up on her lap."

They enjoyed a peaceful half hour passing through small rural communities where old men sat on park benches and children played on swings. Dottie knew from her many years in the business that the cost of real estate in this area was cheap compared with the city of Toronto and its suburbs, and she wondered if she should consider a move to one of these villages when she retired. She could make new friends and get involved in community activities. An image of her playing bingo at a charity function or making apple pies for a bake sale squashed that idea. She admired friends who enjoyed these activities, but they weren't for her.

Just as they were rounding a bend in the road, Dottie caught a flash of metal in the side mirror. She looked back and saw a Harley motorbike hurtling toward them. Her throat constricted when she recognized the rider. "Mabel, it's Billy! He's right behind us!"

Mabel pushed the accelerator down hard, and the car shot forward. She negotiated a curve in the road with great skill, but just as the road straightened, a truck loomed ahead of them. An oncoming van made it impossible for Mabel to overtake the truck, and she slammed on the brakes. Tires screeching, the car spun off the road and headed straight towards a tree.

***

Dottie slowly opened her eyes and glanced over at Mabel. "Are you all right?"

"I feel as though a steamroller has just been driven over me!" Mabel groaned. "What about you?"

"I've got a cut on my forehead. I'll likely end up with some nasty bruises as well."

"I daren't think what might have happened if I'd hit that van!"

A man stuck his head over the side window. "Are you okay? I've just called 911."

"We're fine," Mabel responded, "but what about my car?"

"Never mind about the car!" Dottie snapped. "Let's get out of here before it explodes!"

The man helped them climb out. Dottie glanced at the driver's side of the Porsche. Apart from some scratches, she couldn't see any damage.

"I was in my truck two vehicles back from you." He looked at Mabel with admiration. "I don't know how you managed to avoid a head-on smash with that van. You're quite the driver."

Mabel beamed. "Thank you."

"I don't suppose you noticed a guy on a motorbike," Dottie broke in. "He was right behind us."

"I did. He drove off in a big hurry."

"That figures."

Shading her eyes, Mabel peered at the car. "I wonder if there's any damage on the passenger side."

The man walked over to look. He returned, shaking his head. "It's caved right in."

Mabel's face fell. "Oh, no, my little car's ruined!"

"It's only a car," Dottie sparked. "You could have killed us!"

The man cleared his throat. "I'll be in my truck if you need me."

As soon as he left, Mabel muttered, "It's that gangster's fault! If he hadn't been chasing us...."

Dottie cut in. "That's right, blame someone else! If you hadn't been driving at breakneck speed, this accident could have been avoided!"

"I always speed, so that's irrelevant," Mabel snapped. "I had to swerve to avoid that van—that was a neat bit of driving, let me tell you!"

"So neat that you drove into a tree!" Mabel gave Dottie the blackest look. "And while we're on the subject," Dottie continued, "never mind the dent and scratches on the car. That old jalopy of yours is in bad shape. Apart from problems with the brakes, there's a clunking noise coming from the gearbox. It's high time you invested in a new car."

"What do you know about cars?" Mabel bristled. "All you do is take your fancy BMW to the dealer and have them check it over. They might be overcharging you or charging you for repairs they didn't carry out. You wouldn't have a clue!"

"At least I stick to the speed limits!"

"You drive like a wimp!"

"I drive defensively!" Dottie shot back, her face hot with anger.

"Is that what you call it!"

Dottie stuck her face into Mabel's. Dropping her voice to almost a whisper, she hissed, "I've had it with your crappy car and your dangerous driving. I'm never getting into a car with you again!"

"That's fine by me! I wasn't planning to ask you!"

CHAPTER 5

D ottie was so upset over her argument with Mabel that she'd quite forgotten about her date with Fred Fortune, until she stepped into her bedroom to change into something more comfortable for being miserable about the house. There, laid out on her bed, were the skirt and blouse she'd planned on wearing.

"Shoot!" she muttered. "What was I thinking? I promised myself to make a serious effort to find the right man, and I'm going out for dinner with a middle-aged hippie!"

A quick glance at the clock confirmed she had time for a bath. In fact, she had plenty of time to get ready. All she really lacked was enthusiasm. Fred was not a promising prospect. Oh, he looked spry enough. All his moveable parts were probably still working, and he seemed to have a good sense of fun, but... well, he'd turned up on her doorstep a week ago, after an absence of forty years, in a moth-eaten T-shirt, jeans, and battered cowboy boots so scuffed that the leather was barely visible. Strands of grey hair escaped from a ponytail held together with an elastic band.

"You don't know who I am, do you?" he'd teased.

You got that one right, she thought. *Not a clue.*

He grinned. "Remember Woodstock?"

Memories had floated back. Dottie and a girlfriend had driven down to Yasgur's farm in a genuine Volkswagen Beetle decorated with stick-on daisies, no less. They arrived outside Woodstock, New York, to find themselves in the only all-hippie traffic jam in world history. That's where she'd met Fred.

41

He'd wandered over and introduced himself to them, making some lame joke about not knowing which was in worse shape—his bike or their car. He wore a beaded shirt tucked into tight-fitting blue jeans. Brown, sun-streaked hair hung loosely on his shoulders. With his deep tan and gorgeous blue eyes, Dottie had fallen for him on the spot.

Surely, this sorry-looking creature in front of her couldn't be Fred, she'd thought. She took a good look at him. There was no doubt about it. The figure had changed, but the eyes were as blue and sparkling as ever.

"How did you find me?"

"Easy. Just looked up 'Flowers' in the phone book. There was only one 'D. Flowers' listed, so I took a chance."

Too bad she'd gone back to her birth name when she'd divorced Roger Wilmot.

"How long have you been in Canada?" Dottie had been tempted to say that the last time they'd spoken he'd been on his way to San Francisco, but she decided not to open old wounds.

"More than fifteen years. I lived in Alberta until a couple of years ago." He held up a bottle of red wine. She recognized the label. They'd drunk this cheap brand of wine in great quantities at Woodstock while watching Joan Baez and Credence Clearwater Revival.

Dottie invited Fred into the house. Within minutes, he opened the bottle and poured them each a glass.

"Did we really drink this awful stuff?"

"Yeah, it's hard to believe, isn't it?"

The familiar vinegary taste had taken her back to those crazy days in August 1969. They planned to camp out under the stars. In reality, they had three days of little or no sleep. It rained relentlessly, and they'd been ankle deep in mud most of the time. The toilets overflowed; the food ran out; but nothing could dampen her spirits. She was with Fred and, for three days, nothing else had mattered.

Fred was born and raised in Boston. "I'm not going home," he'd told a tearful Dottie once the festival closed. "My family don't know it yet, but I'm going to San Francisco." He'd held her close for a long moment. "I'll write."

When she returned to Montreal, Dottie had taken sick. A severe cold developed into pneumonia, so she stayed home for several weeks. Each night, she dreamt about Fred and frequently woke up in the middle of the night in tears. Each morning, she listened for the mail carrier, praying for a letter. It never came. Several months later, she joined in the social whirl of Montreal's nightlife and met her future husband shortly afterwards.

***

Now, Dottie climbed out of the bath and wrapped herself in a large bath towel. As she smoothed antiwrinkle cream on her skin, her mind raced. They'd eat and talk about old times, and then she would tell him, gently of course, that she already had a man in her life. That should do the trick. She had no qualms about telling a lie every now and then, particularly if it got her out of ticklish situations.

Dottie put on the Liz Claiborne denim skirt with red embroidered flowers on the hem and the white peasant blouse. She applied a touch of red lipstick and swirled around in front of the long mirror, long hair falling over her shoulders. For a fleeting moment, she felt eighteen again.

Fred arrived promptly at seven with a box of chocolates. Dottie spotted a tag that showed they'd been on special at Wal-Mart, but the chocolates were a nice gesture. He wore black slacks, white shirt, and a tweed jacket—and a decent pair of shoes, polished. Even though he still had his hair in a ponytail, he'd tied it back neatly. He looked quite attractive, reminding her of why she'd once been crazy about him.

They drove into the city in Fred's ancient Volvo. To Dottie's surprise, he pulled up in front of Monsoon, an Indian restaurant noted for its excellent vegetable curries. He *remembers I'm a vegetarian*, thought Dottie, secretly pleased.

As soon as they'd given the waiter their order, Fred asked her about Toronto. "I know almost nothing about the city," he explained. As Dottie told him about the city's attractions, she wondered, did Fred really want to learn more about Toronto or was this just a way to avoid awkward questions, such as why he hadn't written to her?

Later, he took Dottie to a club where they listened to a band play sixties music. Most of the patrons appeared to be in their late fifties. Some men wore bandanas and jeans, and almost everyone smoked. They wouldn't be able to smoke in clubs for much longer with new bylaws coming in. She tried to remember the brand of cigarettes they'd smoked at Woodstock—when they weren't smoking pot.

Fred's voice broke into her reminiscences. "What are you thinking about?"

"Those cheap cigarettes we smoked and marijuana."

He grinned. "You mean these."

He offered her a cigarette, and she recognized the package. "Marlboros!" She took one. "Thanks, I'm surprised you still smoke them."

He lit her cigarette. "I don't. I picked these up for old times' sake."

She took a long drag. "Remember those guys walking through the crowds calling out, 'hash, acid, marijuana' as though it were candy floss!"

Fred leaned back in his chair and blew out a smoke ring. "The air was thick with pot; no wonder we were all high.

The cops must have wondered how in the world they could bust half a million pot smokers."

As the music grew louder, talking became impossible, so they waited until the band took a fifteen-minute break. Fred looked at her through a haze of smoke. "You wonder why I never wrote to you."

His words caught her off guard. "Oh, that was so long ago, I'd forgotten."

"You're a poor liar, Dottie Flowers."

Trying to make her voice sound casual, she asked, "As a matter of interest, Fred, why didn't you write?"

"I lost the piece of paper with your address on it. Sounds dumb, I know, but it's true."

She felt tempted to ask him if he'd ever heard of a phone book. "In the restaurant, you were about to tell me why you came to Canada in the first place, but we got sidetracked."

"I spent the best part of twenty years travelling and working in different parts of the world. About two years ago, I landed in Mexico." He paused. "I got into a spot of trouble."

"What kind of trouble?"

"I ended up in prison for bootlegging."

"Bootlegging! I thought that happened in the twenties during Prohibition."

He slugged down some beer. "After my release, I came to Canada. I had friends in Alberta. They urged me to visit, and I stayed. Loved the place. I found a job with a good-sized legal firm in Calgary, settled down, and raised a family there." As he stared into space, Dottie saw the pain in his eyes.

She decided to avoid questions about his family. "So, you're a lawyer."

"Yep, got my law degree a few years after Woodstock."

"Are you still practicing?"

"I haven't practiced for more than five years." He squished out the cigarette stub in an ashtray. "It's a long story. I'd rather not get into it right now." His hands shook a little as he lit another cigarette.

Dottie decided they'd had enough serious talking for one day. She told him about her friend Mabel and made him laugh describing some of their escapades. His laughter stirred up memories, and Dottie began to wonder if the relationship was worth reviving. Maybe she shouldn't be too hasty in telling him she had someone else. She was about to suggest they get tickets to see Neil Young when he asked her if he could borrow two thousand dollars.

"Two thousand dollars!"

Fred leaned across the table, his eyes pleading. "Look, Dottie, I got mixed up in some shady business dealings, and I've got myself into heavy debt. The thing is I was forced to borrow from a… moneylender."

Her heart sank. The wine, the chocolates, and the dinner were nothing but a ploy to get her to "lend" him some money.

She'd noted the hesitation in his voice. "What kind of moneylender?"

"A loan shark."

Dottie froze. She'd just finished reading a story about a man who didn't make his repayments on time. A passerby found him on the shore of the lake near harbourfront, shot to death.

"What did you do a dumb thing like that for! Loan sharks are ruthless people…"

Fred cut in. "I didn't have any choice."

She did some fast thinking. "The thing is, Fred, I don't have much cash," she lied, crossing her fingers under the table. "I'll give you what I can, but you mustn't get in touch with me again. I'm engaged to be married, and... Jim's a very possessive type."

Even though she would probably never see the money again, Dottie arranged for him to drop by her house in the morning before she went to work. She would give him one thousand dollars. That should stave off the sharks for a while.

In a barely audible voice, Fred said, "Thanks, Dottie. You'll get every penny back, I promise you."

***

A dryness in her throat reminded Dottie that she shouldn't have smoked so many Marlboros. Still, she'd enjoyed the evening, until Fred wrecked it by asking her for money. If she'd had any sense, she'd have sent him packing; but when she saw the desperation in his eyes, she didn't have the heart to refuse.

Dottie picked up a nail file and attacked a hangnail. She didn't relish the idea of going through the rest of her life without a partner. Mabel kept urging her to join a singles club or get involved in the local church, but neither of those organizations appealed. So, for now, she put her energy into her real estate business, enjoyed an occasional Scotch, and ogled Dan, her part-time gardener and handyman. With his blond, shoulder-length hair, his rippling muscles, tight blue jeans or, in the summer, jean cutoffs, he oozed sex appeal. Since he was twenty years her junior, there was no harm in looking, or in Dottie's case, fantasizing.

She needed to find someone about her own age, or a bit younger, fit, attractive, attentive, who would take her to the theatre and maybe the opera, which would give her a chance to wear the designer outfits she loved to buy

47

but seldom had a chance to wear. Her friend Mabel met men at a bridge club and at the local hospital where she volunteered. She dated occasionally, but wasn't really interested in meeting anyone special. Widowed ten years ago, no one since had measured up to her dear Alf.

***

At seven sharp the next morning, Fred drove his Volvo onto Dottie's driveway. She spotted her next door neighbour Gert peering through the kitchen window. *I bet she's dying to know who's calling at this hour of the morning.*

Dottie handed Fred an envelope. He mumbled his thanks and returned to the car. As he drove away, Dottie felt the weight lift from her shoulders. That would be the last she'd see of him, with a bit of luck, anyway. She lit a cigarillo and took a deep drag.

A cup of strong black coffee would go down well right now. Just as she switched on the percolator, the doorbell rang. Gert stood on the doorstep, clutching a milk jug, her mouth twitching into as near to a smile as she could muster. "I wonder if I could bother you for a drop of milk. I've run out. I usually ask Nellie Yokes down the street, but she's away visiting her sister in Kitchener. Larry likes milk in his morning tea."

Dottie wondered what the woman really wanted. She never visited, except to complain about Muggins. "Of course, come in."

She followed Dottie into the bungalow. "I saw you had a visitor, so I knew you were up."

So, that's why Gert came over. "That was a friend of mine."

"Oh." Gert's eyes glittered in anticipation. Dottie almost said that he'd dropped by to pick up his toothbrush and shaving kit but thought better of it. It would only make a bad situation worse. But then again...

Her cell phone rang. "Excuse me, Gert," she said, picking up the phone. The man she'd shown houses to the day before wanted to put in an offer. She put her hand over the mouthpiece. "I can't chat now; I must deal with this phone call."

Gert's face fell. She marched towards the door.

"Don't forget your milk!" Dottie called out, but Gert was already halfway down the garden path.

The call ended. Dottie poured herself a mug of coffee, relieved that Gert had left. The woman had only dropped by for some milk, hoping to pick up a bit of gossip, all quite innocent, so why did she feel uneasy in Gert's presence?

CHAPTER 6

The disastrous date with Fred Fortune made Dottie realize what a fool she'd been to date such a loser. From now on, she'd be very particular about any man she dated. Determined not to dwell on things, Dottie buried herself in work. Fortunately, the real estate business kept her well occupied. Thankful for the distraction, she tried to put all thoughts of the past week out of her mind.

She hoped they'd seen the last of Billy and Den because just the thought of them made her shudder. She'd placed the envelope containing the jewelry behind the mirror at the back of her dresser and secured it with tape. Of course, she'd have to take it to the police, but she would have to answer awkward questions, such as why George Fernandes would put the jewelry in *her* jacket pocket. It would all come out that she and George spoke at the casino and that they'd known each other years ago. Perhaps the police would think she was his accomplice!

***

Thursday afternoon, Serena, Dottie's young receptionist, popped her head around the door. Her short red hair stuck up in all directions as if she'd had an electric shock. "There's someone here to see you." The stress that Serena placed on the word *someone* made Dottie look up in alarm. "Oh, nothing to worry about," Serena reassured her. "It's just that he's so good-looking. A bit old, though—50, maybe more."

"What does he want?" Dottie's hand involuntarily moved to her hair. She smoothed back loose strands and patted the neat bun at the nape of her neck.

Serena's green eyes, made greener with thick eye shadow, popped wide open. "You. I mean, he said that he needed to speak with you personally. He wants to buy some property. That's all he said."

Intrigued, Dottie instructed Serena to invite the visitor into her office. "And no eavesdropping!" she warned.

She drew in a sharp breath when she recognized the man who'd trod on her foot at the spa reception desk. What a coincidence! On closer inspection, she could see from the lines on his face and touches of grey hair that he was probably in his mid-50s. His velvety brown eyes crinkled as he smiled at her. "Senora Flowers, thank you for allowing me to see you on such short notice." They shook hands. "My name is Enrique Garcin. Please call me Enrique. Mr. Garcia is much too formal."

Spanish, eh! She should have persevered with Spanish lessons at night school.

Even though he was Spanish, Dottie couldn't detect an accent. Maybe he was born in Canada. "I'm Dottie Flowers," she said. "We've met before."

His eyes became wary. "I think you must be mistaken…"

"You trod on my foot at Warrendale Spa."

"Ah! Of course!" Was it her imagination, or did he sound relieved? "Your foot is all right?"

"Yes."

"I am glad." He swept his arm towards the chair in front of her desk. "May I?"

"Of course."

He sat down. "I will explain the reason for my visit in a moment. First, allow me to compliment you on the reputation your company has built up over the past five years."

It has a solid reputation but lacks pizzazz a colleague told her when she bought the business three years ago. Since Dottie took over, the company had expanded, and she'd opened another branch in Etobicoke. *The man's been doing his homework*, she thought.

"Thank you, Mr.... Enrique. Now, how can I help you?"

He leaned forward. "I am interested in purchasing a condominium in Toronto at Harbourfront. I would like you to arrange for me to view some models over the next few days, if that is possible." He paused. "I should explain that I am in a hurry because my... my niece, Graciana, is going to start university in September and needs a place to live."

It occurred to Dottie that not too many young students lived in such luxury while they attended university. "I'm sure I can arrange that."

"I might be interested in purchasing a small condo for myself later in the year. My house is too big since my wife..." His voice trailed away.

"I'll do what I can to help."

Enrique uncurled himself from the chair. "I have a tennis match at three, so I must leave."

He had to be at least six foot two. She wondered what he looked like in his tennis gear. She imagined muscular arms executing a perfect ace, and long powerful legs stretching to smash his opponent's 100 mph forehand shot.

"Here is my business card. Call me at any time, day or evening." His eyes swept over her. "I look forward to working with you, Senora Flowers."

"Please call me Dottie."

"Of course."

When the door closed behind him, Dottie sank back in the chair and blew out a long breath. She felt the edge of the business card in her hand, put on her glasses, and scrutinized it. Enrique Garcia, it read, Jewelry Appraiser. A knock on the door made her sit straight up in the chair. She adjusted the rhinestone-framed glasses that had slipped to the tip of her nose. "Come in."

Serena walked in with a cup of coffee and a face full of anticipation. "Well?"

"Well what? He wants to buy a condominium in Toronto, and he's in a hurry to find one. That's all."

"Hmm," Serena said and left with a smirk on her lips.

Dottie peeked again at the card. Jewelry appraiser, huh? A working relationship with the gorgeous Enrique could turn out to be very interesting—very interesting, indeed.

***

The following morning, Dottie managed to line up several condominiums for sale at Harbourfront. Before dialling Enrique's number, she lit a cigarillo to calm an unexpected attack of the jitters.

As she listened to the phone ring, Dottie took a long drag of the cigarillo, figuring she'd be leaving a message. Enrique answered the phone. "Good morning, Dottie."

She started coughing. Fortunately, a few sips from the glass of water on her desk stopped the irritation. "Sorry about that."

"Are you all right?"

Dottie's cigarillo fell out of her fingers onto the carpet. Damn! She stooped to pick it up. "Yes, it's... allergies." Clearing her throat, she tried to sound as businesslike as possible. "I have three condominiums for you to view in Harbourfront. We can see one of them at two-thirty this afternoon and the others tomorrow morning."

"That is excellent!"

"I'll pick you up at one," she said. "What's your address?"

"Let me drive you into the city."

Tempted to take up his offer, she reminded herself this was business. "No, I'll do the driving if you don't mind."

"As you wish. I will meet you at your office to make it easy for you."

"There's no need..."

"I insist." Enrique lowered his voice. "I have an idea. Why don't we have lunch before we look at the condominium? The restaurant I have in mind is within walking distance of Harbourfront."

"If we're back in Harbourfront before three."

"Of course. I will be at your office by eleven-thirty."

As Enrique hung up, Dottie glanced at her watch—ten thirty already! She ran her hands through her hair. "I'm driving Enrique—Mr. Garcia—into Toronto to view a condominium," she told Serena, trying to sound matter-of-fact. "We're going out for lunch first."

Dottie pulled a face as she looked down at her navy slacks and dull grey sweater. She headed for the door. "If it were me," she heard Serena say in a low husky voice, "I would wear the black silk."

Dottie stopped in her tracks and looked at Serena sitting at her desk, hands folded across her ample bosom. "The black silk?"

"Musky perfume, black stockings, and those killer high-heel sandals of yours."

Dottie leapt into her BMW and drove the short distance home. It took a frantic five minutes of searching through her wardrobe before she found a soft lacy blouse to go with the black silk suit. Sheer black stockings and three-inch heel sling backs completed the ensemble. After half a minute of deliberation, she put caution to the wind, pulled her hair out of its bun, and let it fall around her face. She sprayed on Opium perfume and applied wine-coloured lipstick. With ten minutes to spare, she had time for a quick smoke. Remembering the television ad for smokers' breath, she found a packet of mints and chewed on those instead. She took one last glance in the full-length mirror, grabbed her car keys from the kitchen table, and left.

***

Dottie didn't know much about cars, but she recognized a Jaguar when she saw one. The silver-grey beauty rolled to a stop in front of her office. Enrique unfolded himself from the driver's seat and climbed out. Dottie and Serena watched as he strolled towards the door in a black leather jacket, deep blue shirt, and navy slacks.

Serena's eyes were popping out of her head. She chewed hard on a piece of gum. "My, oh my, Dottie, that's what I call eye candy. Just as well it's lunch he's taking you for and not dinner."

"This is a business lunch, Serena, not a date!" Dottie retorted. As the door opened, she whispered anxiously into Serena's ear. "How do I look?"

"Very sexy!"

Casting Serena a dirty look, Dottie turned to greet Enrique. She reached out to shake his hand, but he took hold of her fingers and lifted them to his lips. His eyes met hers. "You look very elegant, Dottie. I look forward to our outing." Dottie felt her face burn. He took her by the arm, and as they headed to the door, from the corner of her eye, Dottie saw Serena give a fist pump.

CHAPTER 7

T raffic clogged the highway, so it took Dottie longer than usual to drive into the city. Finding a parking spot near the restaurant, she looked forward to a relaxing lunch. Enrique escorted her into the restaurant where the maitre d' greeted them. "I have your table reserved, Senor Garcia." He smiled at them. "Please follow me."

The table, set with white linen and gold napkins and a centrepiece of ivory-coloured roses, looked elegant but understated. Spanish-sounding music played softly in the background.

"Would you care for a drink?" Enrique asked. As he looked at her, she noticed a faint scar on his chin. *I wonder how he got that. A street fight in his youth perhaps...*

"Dottie?"

"Oh, sorry, I'll have a glass of white wine, please."

Enrique glanced at the waiter who hovered behind him. "What do you suggest, Manuel?"

"I recommend a Godello," Manuel declared. "It is tangy and dry but light bodied, perfect for lunch."

Their drinks were served within minutes. As she sipped the wine, Dottie remembered that Mabel sometimes stayed the night with her after they had drunk a little too much Chardonnay. She thought about the fun that they'd had since they'd met just over a year ago. She sighed.

Enrique's eyes were full of concern. "Something is troubling you."

"No." Dottie took another sip of wine. "Well, yes, I was thinking about my friend, Mabel Scattergood."

"Is she unwell?"

"No... well, I hope not. We had a big argument." Dottie found herself telling Enrique about the accident and Mabel's distress over her damaged car. "She seemed more upset about her precious car than the fact that we might have been killed."

"Ah, I see. It is a new car?"

"Lord, no! It's an ancient Porsche. And it's in bad shape. I keep telling her she needs to invest in a new one. Even her friends at the Richgreen Golf Club nag her about it. She has lunch there every Wednesday and tries to arrive late so they don't see the car!"

Enrique smiled sympathetically. "An attractive woman like you shouldn't worry about such things. I'm sure you will soon be friends again."

"I doubt it. Mabel can be very stubborn."

Manuel appeared at their table with his notepad. "Let me tell you about our salad special of the day. Our chef has prepared a roasted red pepper and aubergine salad. The sautéed aubergines are served with a tomato sauce made with tomatoes from our own garden and seasoned with a selection of herbs."

Dottie's mouth watered. "That sounds delicious."

"I'll have the paella, please."

"Very good." As he turned to go, Manuel smiled. "I'll remember the extra clams this time, Senor Garcia."

Once the lunch order had been taken, Enrique leaned across the table and took Dottie by the hand. She tried to pull away, but he held on. "Today, we will enjoy our lunch and perhaps learn a little more about each other."

"That's fine by me."

"I need to learn about condominiums," Enrique continued. "If I'm going to be an owner, it is a good idea to be informed, is it not?"

"Of course."

"So tomorrow, I would like to take you out for dinner."

"Dinner?" *He's not backwards in coming forwards,* thought Dottie. Still, why not? Being taken out for dinner by a handsome escort sounded very appealing. She would bring along articles on condominium lifestyles and show him plans of future developments. And if he decided to buy one, they would have something to celebrate.

After lunch, they viewed the condo, as arranged. "It's not what I had in mind," he observed. "It's a little too fancy for my taste."

"I think the ones you'll see tomorrow will be more to your liking."

***

The following morning, Dottie drove to the city to meet Enrique at Harbourfront. She'd dressed with care, choosing a tailored navy blue suit, mustard-coloured satin blouse, and her favourite earrings with large amber stones. When the Jaguar pulled up, Dottie saw someone in the passenger seat. Enrique climbed out of the car, rushed to the passenger side, and opened the door. A curvaceous blonde in a hot pink T-shirt and a figure-hugging white skirt climbed out. She wore heavy eye makeup and bright pink lipstick. Mid-30s, Dottie guessed. "Dottie, this is my— er—my niece, Graciana Garcia. Graciana, this is Dottie Flowers." Beads of sweat had broken out on his forehead.

Dottie smiled. "I'm pleased to meet you."

Graciana glanced briefly at Dottie. "Hi." She fumbled in her purse and popped a piece of gum into her mouth.

They rode the elevator to the thirty-sixth floor in silence. Once they were in the condo, Graciana excused herself. "I'm going to check out the master bedroom ensuite." High-heeled sandals clicked as she marched across the hardwood floor.

"This is so embarrassing," Enrique said. "I must apologize for not letting you know about Graciana. She decided at the last minute she wanted to come."

"It doesn't matter. She'll be living in the condo, so she should have a say in which one you choose."

That didn't seem to reassure Enrique. He paced back and forth, dabbing his forehead with a handkerchief. Graciana reappeared, hands on hips. "The ensuite is the size of a coat closet," she complained. "Let's look at the other model."

"Yes, yes, of course. Dottie, would you mind?"

"Of course not. It's a two-bedroom on the fiftieth floor."

Graciana seemed quite taken with the two-bedroom condo with its breathtaking view of the harbour and islands. When she waltzed over to the window for another look at the view, Enrique took Dottie to one side. "About dinner," he spoke quietly, his eyes focused on Graciana. "Could we change it to Thursday evening instead?"

Dottie hadn't any plans. "No problem."

Graciana turned away from the window, a half smile on her lips. "Uncle Enrique, we have to leave, I have a manicure at 4:00. You said you'd drop me off at the salon."

***

Dottie watched as Enrique backed the Jaguar out of its parking spot. Something didn't add. Over lunch, Enrique had been full of self-confidence and oozed charm. Around the demanding Graciana, he acted like a bowl of jelly. Why he would be so nervous around his niece? Apart from that,

Graciana looked more Scandinavian than Spanish. And wasn't she a bit old to be a student? Perhaps Dottie would find out more Thursday night over dinner if Graciana didn't decide to tag along.

***

Enrique phoned the next day to cancel the dinner engagement. "I am so sorry, my dear. Something urgent has come up, so I cannot take you out for dinner." Something urgent. It's probably Graciana demanding that he drive her to some club or other. "I do have some good news. I have decided to put in an offer for the two-bedroom condo."

"That's great."

"We can talk about that later." He paused. "Do you like opera?"

Fond memories of attending the opera with her ex-husband, before she found out he was an embezzler, popped into her head. "Yes, I do."

"I have two tickets for the opening night of *La Boheme* next Friday. I would like you to be my guest."

CHAPTER 8

Enrique's invitation to the opera delighted Dottie, since it gave her the opportunity to wear one of her new outfits. Just a month ago, she'd scouted Holt Renfrew well ahead of a sale and found a Versace dress and an Armani dress and jacket. As she rooted through the closet, Dottie found an old velvet box. Curious, she opened it and discovered the red stone pendant and matching ring left to her by a dear aunt. She removed the red silk Versace dress from its garment bag and held the pendant next to it. Perfect!

Enrique arrived promptly at 7:00, his dark good looks enhanced by a black tuxedo and wine-coloured cummerbund. He took Dottie's hand. "You look stunning, my dear. Your outfit is most becoming."

For a moment, Dottie saw something in his eyes that didn't fit the image. He looked as if he regretted something and felt the urge to fess up. Had he changed his mind about the condo? "Is everything all right? You look a bit worried."

"Oh, yes, everything is going very nicely," he hastened to assure her. "Here, let me help you with your stole." The silky fabric had slipped off her shoulders. As he replaced the stole, Enrique became quite still. His eyes were fixed on the pendant around her neck. "That pendant is exquisite."

Dottie explained that her aunt had bequeathed it to her. "It goes with my ring," she added, holding out her right hand for Enrique to see.

Enrique took a deep breath. "I hope you have them insured. They're worth quite a lot of money."

"Are you serious? I thought they were just costume jewelry." She looked closely at the pendant. "I worked in a jewelry store one summer when I was in high school. I thought I could tell real gems from fake."

"Sometimes, it's obvious, but I've seen fake stones so expertly crafted they are hard to distinguish from the real thing." He paused. "Those are genuine rubies. As jewelry is my business, I will be happy to appraise them for you."

"Thank you. I might take you up on that."

"I do hope so. Now, my dear, let's go and enjoy the evening." He took her by the arm. "*La Boheme* is one of my favourite operas. Did you know that…" Dottie half listened as he explained about the history of the opera. He sounded like his old self again, but she couldn't help wondering what had been troubling him when he'd arrived at the house.

***

The following week, real estate business kept Dottie occupied, so she didn't have time to wonder about Enrique. Her Friday evening appointment had been cancelled at the last minute, and Dottie planned to make the most of the unexpected free time. Arriving home, she changed from her pinstriped navy suit into casual slacks and a sweater. She decided to treat herself to a Scotch before preparing dinner.

The phone rang. Dottie groaned inwardly when she recognized Yolanda's deep voice. "Hello, Dottie." In typical Yolanda style, she got right to the point. "Aunt Mabel told me that you might be interested in riding lessons. We have a senior special starting this Monday at Morrison's. The lessons are half price." Yolanda owned Morrison's Riding Academy and ran the stables like a sergeant major according to friends who'd taken lessons there. About to make an excuse, Dottie remembered how much she'd enjoyed riding as a young girl. She'd often thought of taking it up again; the winery ride had reminded her how much she missed being around horses. Before Dottie had a chance to say anything, Yolanda continued, "It's a good deal, and I've only got one opening left."

"I'll sign up."

"Good." Yolanda paused. "About you and Aunt Mabel." *Oh, here we go,* thought Dottie. "When are the two of you going to stop being so stubborn and be friends again?"

"These things take time, Yolanda."

"Remember, it's harder to mend fences if you leave it too long."

"I agree. Look, I really must be going…"

"I must rush as well. I have a lesson in five minutes. I'll see you on Monday. Don't be late. The lesson begins promptly at two."

By force of will, Dottie managed to resist slamming down the phone. "Goodbye, Yolanda."

She poured herself a healthy shot of Scotch over ice. Sipping the ice-cold liquid, she thought about the phone call. Although Dottie never made decisions without careful thought, she'd committed herself to a set of riding lessons. These days, even though she exercised three times a week, her limbs were stiff when she got out of bed. She hated to admit it, but she had aches and pains in her joints that no amount of exercising could cure. Drink in hand, she sat down on the sofa. Muggins jumped up beside her and settled down for a nap. This is what a woman of my age should be doing, she told herself. Taking it easy, not dashing off to the countryside to ride horses!

Her thoughts drifted back to when she was 11 and horse crazy. Drawn by the sight of children learning to ride in the paddock behind her home, Dottie would sit on the fence to watch, her long hair in plaits, wearing an old pair of jodhpurs a cousin had outgrown. One day, the instructor had invited Dottie to help groom the horses, and as payment, offered her a free lesson. From the moment she'd mounted the pony, Dottie had been hooked.

Dottie smiled. It would feel good to be around horses again, even though it meant seeing Yolanda every week.

***

She told Enrique about the lessons.

"I didn't know you were interested in horses." He tapped his finger on his lips. "I'm free on Monday afternoon, so I'll drive you up there. I am a regular client at Morrison's. I might go for a short ride while I wait for you."

The seniors' beginner group watched as teenagers led horses, saddled and bridled, out of the stables. Yolanda assigned a horse to each rider, and with the help of an assistant, she demonstrated how to mount. Laughing nervously, the group struggled to follow her example. Dottie climbed on her little bay horse with ease. As she did so, she noticed a man in a brown tweed riding jacket in front of her. He took his horse's reins, placed his left foot in the stirrup, and swung into the saddle. Dottie watched as he deftly adjusted the strap of his right stirrup. Once they were all mounted, Yolanda waved her crop in the air, and the teenagers led the horses towards the riding arena.

As they entered, Dottie saw a man in a grubby jean jacket chatting with Enrique. The jacket had a Harley-Davidson insignia on it. Craning her neck to see the man's face, she jumped when Yolanda's strident voice called out. "Heels down, toes up!" Dottie's horse, Pedro, had a round stomach and sleepy eyes. "He's an old horse, ideal for a beginner," Yolanda assured Dottie. "Just relax. He won't hurt a fly."

So, Yolanda thinks I'm nervous around horses, does she! I could show her a thing or two! She took a deep breath. *Just let it go.* Suddenly, Pedro stopped.

"Just squeeze him gently with your knees," a voice suggested in a well-modulated British accent. She turned around. It was the man in the tweed jacket. With his back ramrod straight and a military-style moustache, he looked very aristocratic. Smiling, he touched his riding hat and bowed slightly. "Arnold. Arnold Gateshead."

"Dottie Flowers. Pleased to meet you."

Arnold rode up beside her. "Must apologize for interfering, Mrs. Flowers," he began. "The thing is," he looked around furtively, "I'm here under false pretences."

"What do you mean?"

"I can ride perfectly well. But I want to get to know a certain young woman and decided the best way to make her acquaintance was to take riding lessons."

Dottie glanced around the arena. Surely, he wasn't interested in Yolanda's female assistant! She was very pretty with a slim, curvaceous figure, but couldn't be more than 18. Arnold Gateshead appeared to be in his early 40s.

Yolanda yelled at one rider in her deep contralto voice, "Don't pull on the reins!"

"I wouldn't want to be in his shoes!" Dottie joked, but Arnold wasn't listening. His eyes were riveted on Yolanda.

As if reading her mind, he chuckled. "She's a real looker, isn't she? Would stand out in any crowd."

Yolanda's large body was encased in a red tartan jacket. She slapped her crop against shiny riding boots whenever she barked out an order. Dottie avoided Arnold's eyes when she answered, "She certainly would stand out in a crowd."

"And knows her own mind. Runs her publishing company just as efficiently as she runs her stables. Won't take any nonsense from anyone. I like that in a woman."

Dottie was about to ask him how he knew so much about Yolanda when the woman herself marched over.

"Arnold, please get in line, and concentrate on your lesson." Yolanda glared at Dottie. "And Dottie, you'd do well to follow my directions if I'm ever to make a rider of you!"

Dottie was surprised that this charming, if somewhat old-fashioned, man was making sheep-eyes at the formidable Yolanda, because the woman never failed to raise her hackles.Arnold winked at Dottie before obeying orders.

The remainder of the lesson consisted of riding around the arena in single file, with Yolanda's deep voice ordering everyone to "sit up straight, heels down, toes up!" over and over just like a record. Dottie smiled to herself. Even if the lessons were boring, Arnold's pursuit of Yolanda might prove to be a welcome distraction.

***

"How was the lesson?" Enrique asked Dottie as he drove her home.

"Okay."

Enrique glanced at her. "You don't sound very thrilled."

"It was a bit tedious walking around the arena for an hour. The next lesson should be more interesting since we'll be learning to post."

She watched Enrique as he skilfully drove the Jeep around a sharp bend in the road. She'd been taken by surprise when he'd arrived wearing blue jeans and dark tan cowboy boots at her house in the sporty SUV. "How was your ride?"

"I didn't go. I got... sidetracked by someone."

"The man in the Harley-Davidson jacket?"

Did she imagine it, or did Enrique tighten his grip on the steering wheel? His voice sounded wary. "You know him?"

"He had his back to me, so I couldn't see his face. Does he work for Yolanda?"

"On and off when she needs extra help."

Enrique signalled to turn onto the Queen Elizabeth Highway and merged into the traffic. His brows furrowed as he concentrated on the road. As they headed towards her bungalow, Dottie thought about the way Enrique had tensed up when she'd mentioned the man at the stables. "Why don't we go back to my place. I'll make some coffee." And do some probing, she added to herself.

"What an excellent idea!"

When Enrique found out that Dottie had some whipping cream in the fridge, he insisted on making Spanish coffees. As he served the coffee, his cell phone rang. He excused himself and left the room.

Enrique frowned as he returned to the living room. "I have to go," he said, his voice sounding apologetic.

As the front door closed, she sighed. So much for her plan to find out more about Enrique's connection with the Harley-Davidson guy.

***

By the third lesson, Dottie and Arnold had become friends, or perhaps a better description of their relationship would be "partners in the seduction of Yolanda Paris." Dottie found out that he worked as a banker in London, was a bachelor and was taking an extended vacation at a friend's cottage in Bracebridge. The cottage lay next door to Yolanda's family cottage, and once Arnold had set eyes on her, he'd been smitten. Life at the stables became quite amusing as Arnold tried to get Yolanda's attention. Once, he twisted the stirrup strap around his leg and asked Yolanda's to help him.

"What is this nonsense?"

Arnold blushed. "I do beg your pardon, Y... Miss Paris, I can't think how it could have happened."

As she bent forwards to untwist the stirrup, Arnold leaned towards Yolanda and whispered in her ear. She slapped him across the face. "Mind your manners!" Her face a deep crimson, Yolanda marched away.

Dottie felt the urge to laugh but managed to stifle it. "What did you say to Yolanda?"

Arnold rubbed the side of his face gently as if Yolanda had kissed him, not slapped him. "I told her how becoming she looked in her riding outfit."

"What exactly did you say, Arnold?" Even Yolanda couldn't be offended by that remark.

"Well," he smoothed his moustache. "I did glance down the front of her jacket when she leaned over the stirrup. She's very well endowed. I might have said something about her being a buxom filly."

"No wonder she slapped you, Arnold. You have to be more romantic than that. Why don't you ask her out for dinner?"

Arnold gazed at his riding boots. "I'm afraid she might not accept."

Dottie thought Arnold was probably right. She crossed her fingers behind her back. "Of course, she will."

Arnold looked pleased. "I'll ask her tomorrow."

***

The next Monday, Yolanda, riding a powerful-looking grey horse, led the group out of the arena into a nearby paddock. "This afternoon, you will experience riding in the great outdoors." She brandished her crop in the air, reminding Dottie of Queen Boadicea leading her troops to battle. "We'll trot around the paddock first and then ride through the field. Follow me!"

As they headed into the field, Dottie breathed in the sweet scents of freshly mown grass. With the temperature in the upper seventies, she welcomed the light breeze that fanned across her face. Bees hummed lazily in the sunshine, gathering nectar. Glancing to her right, Dottie noticed a swarm of them hovering around a gorse bush. Suddenly, the horse in front of Arnold whinnied and reared. Jane, a group member, screamed as her horse bolted across the field. Arnold urged his horse into a gallop and raced to her rescue. As the frightened animal neared a fence, Arnold managed to grab the reins.

The two horses came to a halt, their hindquarters gleaming with sweat. Arnold dismounted. He took hold of Jane's hand and spoke to her before helping her to dismount. Dottie grinned. This would make a wonderful picture for the local newspaper. She could see the headlines now: *Knight in Riding Breeches Saves Damsel in Distress*. Yolanda caught up to them and turned to Arnold, her eyes full of admiration.

Later, Dottie spoke with Arnold. "Well?"

"It seems the horse was stung by a bee."

"What did Yolanda have to say?"

"Yolanda worried about repercussions if anything had happened to Jane—legal suits and all that."

"Wasn't she concerned about Jane?"

"What? Oh, I see what you mean." Arnold's face turned pink. "Of course. Made quite a fuss of her and promised to give her a discount off her next set of lessons."

"I expect Yolanda's very grateful to you for the rescue."

He turned to Dottie, his face beaming. "She's done me the honour of accepting an invitation to dinner." He coughed nervously. "It was your idea, and I'm very grateful. Thanks, Dottie."

Did Arnold know what he was doing? When she'd suggested he ask Yolanda for dinner, Dottie hadn't believed for one moment that Yolanda would accept. But the rescue had changed all that.

CHAPTER 9

Dottie attempted several times to snoop around the stables, but somebody was always around. On the day of her final lesson, she decided to take matters into her own hands. Halfway through the lesson, she complained about a headache and excused herself. Dottie had no idea what, or whom, to look for. Enrique had been edgier than ever since she'd begun her riding lessons, and she itched to find out why.

Dottie could hear Yolanda's strident voice across the yard as she walked over to the stables. "Michele, sit up straight! And, Ted, stop pulling on those reins!" When Dottie entered the main building, familiar smells of horse manure, sweet hay, and polished leather brought a flood of memories. She smiled when she spotted the rosettes—blue, red, and yellow—displayed next to an array of saddles and bridles. At 13, she'd won first prize in a local gymkhana and still treasured the blue rosette presented to her that day.

She wandered outside again. The horse stalls faced the yard, and from each of the stall's half doors hung wooden plaques with names painted on them. Dottie stroked the nose of a black mare that poked her head over the half door. "Sorry, Jinks, I haven't got a carrot with me today."

She noticed a young man heaving manure into a wheelbarrow inside Jinks' stall. "It's hard work," Dottie remarked.

He stopped and wiped his hand over his forehead. "It's not too bad. I've only got one more to do, and I'm finished for the day."

She smiled. "I'm Dottie Flowers."

The young man blushed. "Tim –er, Tim Evans."

"I spent most of my teenage years around the local stables."

He leaned on his shovel. "I've been around horses all my life. Mostly smaller stables."

After they'd chatted amiably for a while about their experiences with horses, Dottie decided to get down to business. The lesson would be over soon. It would be awkward if Yolanda caught her chatting away with a stable hand. "How many people work here?"

"I dunno exactly. Two of us are full-time, but she hires part-timers as well."

From the corner of her eye, Dottie saw the man in the jeans jacket, standing near a barn door across the yard. He stood next to another man. Both of them had their backs turned away from her. The second man had long grey hair tied in a ponytail and wore scuffed cowboy boots. Dottie's heart lurched when she saw the metal stars on the boots glint in the sun. Fred Fortune! What was he doing here? At that moment, Fred turned away from his companion and headed towards the car park. She watched him climb into his rusty Volvo and drive away.

Tim's voice broke into her musings. "I must get this stall finished."

"Go ahead."

The midday sun was hot, so Dottie strolled into the cool stable and sat on a hay bale. She had to find an excuse to chat with the man to find out the connection between him and Enrique and Fred Fortune. Maybe it had to do with buying horses, but she didn't think so. It could be racehorses, of course. In Dottie's mind, horseracing was full of criminal types out to make a fast buck.

Suddenly, a voice yelled across the yard. "Tim! I gotta move some hay bales!" Dottie looked up. Hands cupped around his mouth, the man added, "Shouldn't take too long with two of us working at it."

"OK, I'll be right over!"

The man held up his hand in a gesture of thanks and grinned. When Dottie saw his toothless grin, her legs wobbled like jelly. It was Billy Wills, one of the men who had followed her and Mabel from the casino where George Fernandes had been stabbed to death.

Tim poked his head around the stable door. He looked sheepish. "I'm goin' to give that Billy Wills a hand. I don't know why I'm botherin'. He never does a proper day's work."

Dottie tried to keep her voice level. "Has he been here long?"

"A couple weeks this time."

"So, he's been here before."

"Off and on. He'll be leaving the end of the week."

"How do you know?"

"I overheard him talkin' to Miss Paris."

Before Dottie had a chance to glean more information, Tim turned away and headed across the yard.

Fortunately, Dottie had the car keys in her pocket. When the two men disappeared into the stables, she ran to the car and climbed quickly inside. What would have happened if Billy had seen her? She could see how Fred Fortune might be tempted to join forces with the likes of Billy, hoping to make some easy money. But that wasn't her main concern. What could a suave man of the world like Enrique possibly have in common with an unsavoury character such as Billy? And why did Billy work at Yolanda's stables?

It could all be perfectly innocent, she told herself. If so, why did she have an uncomfortable feeling in the pit of her stomach?

***

When Dottie arrived home, she saw the flashing red light on her answering machine. First things first, she decided, pouring herself a small Scotch. Her head still reeling from the shock of seeing Billy, Dottie took a sip of her drink and sat on the sofa. It didn't take long for the smooth blend to work its magic.

She punched in the code and listened to her messages. The first two were business calls. Then, she heard Enrique's husky voice. His words came out in a rush. "I have to go away on business, my dear Dottie. I'll be back next week and will get in touch when I return. I will book a table at Bombay Palace, that new Indian restaurant I spoke of, and take you out for dinner."

Dottie replaced the receiver. *What kind of business*, she wondered. A proverb often quoted by Mabel sprang into her head. *When the cat's away, the mice will play.* If she kept out of Billy's way, Enrique's business trip gave her the perfect opportunity to snoop. She needed to know why Billy worked at Yolanda's stables. Maybe he was using the stables to hide contraband or whatever stolen goods were called.

Dottie put a call through to Morrison's Livery Stables. "I'd like to book four more lessons, please." As she arranged times and dates with an instructor, Dottie's mind raced. Haylofts were the most likely places to hide stolen goods. She would start her search there. It shouldn't be difficult if no one saw her. An image of Billy looming over her as she uncovered boxes of loot made her shudder, and she gulped down the rest of her drink.

***

The opportunity for Dottie to search the hayloft came up unexpectedly. After her first extra lesson, she got into another conversation with Tim Evans. "I suppose the loft's full of hay."

"There are other things up there as well."

Dottie felt her skin prickle. "What other things?"

"Horse feed. Extra rakes and shovels. And some old tack. Usual stuff."

Dottie glanced at the ladder running up the wall to the hayloft. It looked a bit scary, but she'd scaled this kind of ladder many times. "I used to spend hours in the hayloft breaking up bales of hay and tossing it down for the horses." She smiled encouragingly at Tim. "Do you think I could look around?"

"Not sure." Tim looked around furtively, then back at Dottie. His voice became conspiratorial. "I seen that Billy Wills and another fellow carryin' a box up there the other day."

Dottie's heart raced. "What kind of box?"

"A cardboard box, tied with thick string and masking tape."

"You think it might contain something... illegal?"

"I dunno. I just got a feeling they're up to no good, that's all."

"Tim!" Yolanda's deep voice resonated through the stalls. "Where are you? I need your help with getting Lady Jane into a horsebox."

Tim grabbed his jacket. "Coming, Miss Paris!"

Dottie seized this unexpected opportunity. When Tim left, she rushed to the ladder and began to climb. Her legs ached, and her arms felt as if they were being pulled out of their sockets as she struggled up the vertical ladder. Her jacket snagged on a nail at one point, almost throwing her off balance. She'd been 16 the last time she'd scaled a ladder like this. What made her think it would be easy to climb all those years later? She forced herself not to look down and, with a sigh of relief, reached the top.

Two small windows provided enough light for Dottie to look around. In one corner, shovels and rakes were lined up, ready for use. Neatly stacked hay bales filled most of the loft; there didn't seem to be room for a box. She peered in each corner, but nothing seemed out of place. Then, she noticed a half door with an iron handle underneath one window, almost hidden by the hay bales. Dottie glanced through the window. In the yard below, Tim stood behind a horsebox, holding the reins of a skittish grey mare while Yolanda stood to one side, giving orders. The way Lady Jane tossed her head and reared up, it could be a while before they secured her in the box. Removing a flashlight from her pocket, Dottie got down on her haunches.

She gave the iron handle a sharp pull. The door opened, and the flashlight's beam revealed a small dusty storage area, scattered with straw. A large rectangular object covered by a tarpaulin lay near the door. Dottie lifted the edge of the tarpaulin and pulled it back. About two dozen wooden boxes of the same size stood on the floor. They looked as if they'd never been opened. The cardboard box tied with cord and masking tape Tim had described sat next to them. Fortunately, she'd brought a penknife! Taking it from her pocket, a thought occurred to her. If she cut through the cord, Billy would know someone had found the box. It took her a good five minutes to untie the cord and remove the masking tape. Biting her lip, she pried the container open and looked inside.

She opened a small box inside the container and found a diamond necklace and earrings on black velvet. A quick look inside some other boxes revealed more jewelry sets and Rolex watches. She pried open a wooden box and discovered bottles of wine with a Trepaniers label. Her throat went dry when she remembered the newspaper article about the vineyard robbery. Could this be the stolen wine?

Suddenly, she could hear men's voices in the yard. In a panic, Dottie pushed the velvet boxes back into the cardboard container, all thumbs as she tied the cord and secured the masking tape. Billy's voice rang out. "I need to check the loft. I think I left a sweatshirt up there." Dottie heard the clump of boots as he walked into the stables, then the creak as he started to climb the ladder. Heart pounding, she pushed down the lid of the wooden box, dragged the tarpaulin back in place, and closed the storage room door. As she ducked behind some hay bales, dust floated up. She felt a tickle in her throat. *If I cough, the game's over.*

CHAPTER 10

Dottie paced the living room, smoking a cigarillo, pausing once or twice to cough. She really must cut down on her smoking. She'd had a narrow escape this afternoon. Billy had been halfway up the ladder when Tim had come looking for him. A minute later and Billy would have been in the loft. An icy shiver raced down her spine when she thought of what he might have done.

Now, she had other things to worry about. Enrique would be here in ten minutes, and she still hadn't made up her mind what to say to him. Should she confront him or use a more subtle approach?

She practiced aloud. "Enrique, I didn't know that you and Billy Wills were acquainted." No. That sounded too much like a line out of a play. Maybe she should be more direct, look him straight in the eye, and say, "What are you and Billy up to?" No. She didn't have the courage to be that forward. Besides, Enrique would probably clam right up. Dottie plopped herself on the sofa. Taking a long draw on the cigarillo, she inhaled the smoke and blew it out through her nostrils. That felt better.

Another angle might work. "When I was at the stables, I saw a man I recognized. His name is Billy Wills. Do you happen to know whom I'm talking about?" She ran a hand through her hair. No, that wouldn't do, either. Enrique would be on his guard right away.

To make matters worse, Dottie would be away for the next four weeks. Last night, she'd had a frantic phone call from her daughter Hettie in Unionville. Hettie had fallen over a toy truck and broken her right wrist. "The thing is, Mother, Jake's in China on business and won't be back until the end of the month. I don't know how I'm going to manage with the twins. Could you possibly come and stay until Jake gets back?"

She wasn't surprised by Hettie's accident. The twins were allowed to do exactly as they pleased, and so the living room, hallway, and den were always scattered with toys. The thought of spending two weeks in a messy house with whiny children made her feel quite depressed. At least she didn't have to worry about her real estate business. To cut down her hours, Dottie had hired another agent. The decision had been an excellent one, and he would cover her workload while she stayed with Hettie.

Dottie checked her appearance in the hall mirror. What a wreck! Her breath reeked of tobacco; her hair looked like a bird's nest; and she'd dropped ash on her black jersey dress. Finding a strong breath mint in her purse, she sucked on it hard, and then dashed around the room, emptying the ashtrays, hiding the cigarillos, and spraying the room with air freshener. She hadn't told Enrique she smoked. Surely he wouldn't be uptight about it, but she wasn't going to take a chance.

Satisfied that the air freshener had done its job, Dottie changed into her teal silk dress and jacket. The fitted dress enhanced her willowy figure, and the lacy bodice revealed just enough cleavage to tantalize. She dabbed Opium perfume on her wrists. As she brushed her hair, one of Mabel's often-quoted proverbs sprang into her head. *When in doubt, do nothing.* Yes! She would act as if nothing had happened. They would have a drink here, and then go out for a relaxing dinner as planned. *In for a penny, in for a pound,* she thought. Oh dear, she sounded just like Mabel.

***

Enrique arrived half an hour late. Wearing a sand-coloured suede jacket and black silk shirt, he breezed into Dottie's house. Face flushed, he apologized for his tardiness.

"Business problems," he said, flicking his hand in a gesture of dismissal.

As they entered Bombay Palace, a tall man in a white turban greeted them with a smile and bow. The musky smell of incense filled the air. When she heard the hypnotic sound of a flute playing softly in the background, Dottie half expected to see a cobra uncurling from its basket. Richly brocaded cushions decorated the wooden love seats, giving the seats a softer more sensuous look. Candles flickered on the wooden tables, and gold filigree napkin holders in the shape of cobras held silky dark red napkins.

Enrique gave his name to a young woman in a sari hovering near the desk. She scanned the reservations book. "There doesn't appear to be a reservation for you, Mr. Garcia."

Enrique's eyes flashed. "There must a mistake. I made the reservation more than a week ago."

The young woman shook her head. "I'm sorry."

Enrique looked around. He excused himself and walked over to the tall man. After a brief conversation, Enrique took out his wallet, pulled out some dollar bills, and pressed them into the man's palm. *He forgot to book a table*, Dottie surmised. *Now, he has to resort to bribery.*

They were escorted to the back of the restaurant. The maitre d' removed a Reserved sign before seating them at a table set for two. Dottie sank into a gilded chair upholstered in red velvet. Red napkins decorated with gold stars complemented the cream linen tablecloth. "Looks as if we've stolen someone's reserved table," Dottie remarked.

Enrique shrugged. "They have other tables."

They ordered their meal and a selection of Indian dishes and tea with lemon. Once the tea had been served, the tension in Enrique's face eased up a little.

"How was your trip?"

"Trip? Oh, my business trip." He cleared his throat. "It was very... profitable." He smiled and took her hand. "Never mind about me. I want to hear what you've been up to."

"I've been riding."

Enrique's smile faded. "Riding? But you finished your lessons before I went away."

"I had four more."

"And did they help?"

She crossed her fingers in her lap. "Yes. Quite a bit. They've given me more confidence." *More confidence to snoop*, she thought.

Their food was served. Dottie breathed in the exotic aromas of coriander and rich spices. "This looks wonderful."

They concentrated on their meal. After a few mouthfuls, Enrique placed his fork neatly on the plate. His eyes narrowed. "Did you talk to anyone while you were at the stables?"

"I had a few chats with Tim Evans, one of the stable hands."

"Tim is very dependable. Yolanda relies on him for just about everything." Enrique tapped his fingers on the edge of his plate. "Anyone else?"

"No, I didn't speak with anyone else." She took a deep breath. "I saw your friend, the man in the jeans jacket again. This time I saw his face. It was Billy Wills."

Enrique's fingers stopped tapping. His right eye twitched. "How do you know Billy Wills?"

Dottie had never disclosed the George Fernandes business to anyone, and she didn't intend to start now. She had a sudden brainwave. "I met him at a Harley bike sale."

"A Harley bike sale?"

"I like Harley Davidson motorbikes. Anyway, it turns out he wanted to buy an updated model. We got chatting. He talked about a lot of technical stuff, which I didn't understand, but it was fun being up close to a Harley." It wasn't all lies; the part about the bike sale was true.

Enrique's eyebrows furrowed. "That is the only time you've ever come into contact with him?"

"No. We met on a winery trail ride in Niagara a few weeks ago. He was with a couple of his friends." She paused. "What's your connection with Billy Wills, Enrique?"

Enrique dabbed the corners of his mouth with a linen napkin. "We are... partners."

"What kind of partners?"

Enrique settled back in his chair and sipped his wine thoughtfully. Suddenly, he leaned forward, his eyes twinkling. He patted her hand. "You will find out what it's all about very soon, my dear."

"Find out what?"

Enrique tapped the side of his nose with his index finger. "That's all I'm going to say on the matter right now."

"I'll be out of town for the next four weeks. I leave on Sunday." She told him about Hettie's accident.

Enrique drained his glass. "I promise you will know on Saturday."

***

Dottie spent Saturday mornings reading the *Globe and Mail* from cover to cover with a pot of strong black coffee in front of her. As she savoured her first sip of coffee and settled back to read the headlines, the phone rang.

It was her neighbour Margaret. "Dottie, have you seen the local paper?"

"Not yet."

"That serial cat killer has struck again. Two cats this time. Poisoned like the others. I'm trying to keep Tiddles inside." Margaret had recently adopted Tiddles, a tabby kitten, from the Humane Society.

"I wish they'd catch the creep."

"I haven't told you the worst."

"Go on."

"The cats were found in a garden on Greenslade Street."

Dottie bit her lip. Greenslade was just two blocks from their street. She sighed. "Thanks for telling me, Margaret."

As she replaced the receiver, Dottie saw Muggins slink past the sunroom window. He appeared to be stalking something, probably a mouse or a bird. Her stomach clenched. How'd he managed to get out? She positioned a small plate of canned tuna just inside the sunroom door and waited. Within minutes, he bounded around the corner and shot into the house, purring loudly as he settled down to eat. Dottie closed the door with a sigh. Keeping Muggins confined in the house required ingenuity and patience, neither of which Dottie possessed.

The revving of a motorbike caught her attention. Dottie rushed into the living room and looked through the window. With an ear-splitting roar, a Harley zoomed down the street towards her bungalow. The mighty machine turned onto her driveway, and the rider climbed off. He removed his helmet and brushed his hands through dark wavy hair. Even dressed in leather biking gear, Dottie recognized the tall athletic form of Enrique. He'd never looked so good.

Dottie rushed outside. She made her way slowly around the bike, admiring the shiny chrome and the leather saddlebags. "So, you bought yourself a Harley!"

"I told you I would let you know my plans today."

"You did," Dottie breathed. "I never thought it would be this."

Enrique held out a helmet. "Are you coming for a ride?"

"Just try to stop me! I'll go grab a jacket and gloves."

As Dottie rushed off, she saw Gert Bottomley watching her with pursed lips. *I bet she can't wait to run around to tell Nellie Yokes what she'd just witnessed*, Dottie mused. Nellie lived two doors down from Gert, and they were always in and out of each other's homes. How she would love to be a fly on the wall in Nellie's bungalow this morning!

Dottie strapped on the helmet. After Enrique started the Harley, she climbed on behind him. She swung one leg over the smooth leather seat and rested her foot on the pedal, careful to avoid the fiery heat of the exhaust pipe. Wrapping her arms around his waist, she leaned into him, her face pressed against the soft leather of his jacket. He popped the clutch. They raced passed Gert. Dottie caught her eye and couldn't resist giving a thumbs-up sign.

***

The wind whipped in her face as they shot down the Queen Elizabeth Highway. Enrique drove fast, but he knew how to handle the big bike. He wove it skilfully in and out of traffic before exiting the highway onto a country road. She closed her eyes, basking in the warmth of the sun on her back. The thrill she experienced as they dipped around bends and fired up the hills had her heart pounding and brought back memories of that first ride on Fred's bike all those years ago.

They were back in Dottie's driveway thirty minutes later. After she dismounted, Enrique parked and put the kickstand down. He grinned. "Well, how was it?"

Dottie removed the helmet and shook her hair free. "Exciting. Always is. I've leased bikes over the years, but never owned one."

"Why not?"

"It's a long, complicated story. I am thinking of buying one, though."

"I am glad you enjoyed yourself." He pressed the keys into the palm of her hand. "She's all yours."

Dottie's jaw dropped. "What?"

He smiled. "The bike is yours."

"But..."

"It is yours, Dottie. A gift from me. You wondered what I was doing talking with Billy Wills at Morrison's Riding Academy that day. We were settling on a price for the bike." He smiled. "A big deal just came through for me. You are a dear friend, so I wanted to get you something special."

Dottie tried not to let her smile falter, but it was hard. Truth was, they weren't such "dear friends." At least, not yet. And that realization hit harder than the clear fact he was lying.

"It's very generous of you, Enrique, but I can't accept."

"Why not?"

She chewed her lip, "Apart from anything else, I don't have anywhere to keep the bike. My driveway's too small."

"I own a garage two blocks away. You can park the bike there with mine."

"You have a bike! I still don't see..."

Enrique interrupted. "Don't worry, my dear Dottie. I want you to enjoy yourself.Climb on the back again, and we'll take it to the garage now. I left my car there, so we'll park the bike, and I'll bring you home in the car."

He has it all figured out, thought Dottie, as she strapped on her helmet again. A picture of Enrique and Billy deep in conversation at the stables flashed into her head. Bikes might have come into the conversation, but Dottie's instincts told her he and Billy were talking about something much more serious—like stolen jewelry, for example.

Enrique revved up the engine, and the bike moved forward. Dottie closed her eyes and shoved all doubts about Enrique to the back of her mind. A dream of owning her own Harley had come true, and she might as well make the most of it.

CHAPTER 11

Mabel was in a flap. Late for her weekly luncheon at the Richgreen Golf Club, she was about to leave the house when the phone rang. It was Auntie Ada from Australia. Mabel tried to stay focused on her elderly aunt's litany of woes. It wasn't that she didn't care about Uncle Sam's rheumatism; it was just that her aunt tended to repeat herself. Suddenly, Mabel heard a loud crash and glanced through the window. "Oh, Auntie, I must go. My dog's got into our recycling box." After a quick goodbye, she hung up the phone. For once, she was grateful to Fifi, even though it meant cleaning up tin cans scattered over the patio.

Mabel's car hadn't been the same since the accident. True, the dents and scratches were gone, but something about driving it bothered her. Perhaps it reminded her of the fight with Dottie. They hadn't spoken since the day of the accident more than six weeks ago. Whatever the reason, it was time to look around for another car.

Already five minutes late, she pulled into the golf club driveway and climbed out of the car. The luncheon was a casual affair. The group consisted of eight women, but it was taken for granted that, if someone had another engagement, she wouldn't show up. Usually, two or three were missing. In her haste, Mabel dropped her keys.

"Let me help you."

Mabel looked up to find a tall dark-haired man smiling at her. *He looks foreign*, she thought. *Probably French*. "It's my keys. They've fallen under the car." It didn't take him long to reach them. "That's very kind of you," Mabel began.

"Not at all." He paused, and then turned his attention to Mabel's Porsche. "This is a 1986 model, is it not?" He walked around the car, examining it. With his striking good looks, he reminded Mabel of the hero of the paperback romance she'd just finished reading. "It is a beautiful car. It must give you much pleasure."

Mabel blushed. "Oh, yes." She felt sad suddenly. "I was in an accident recently, and it was badly damaged."

The man stopped examining the car and looked at her. "Whoever did the body work must be commended. They did a fine job. Still, an accident can shake one's confidence."

Mabel was pleased that the stranger understood how she felt. "After the car was repaired, I didn't go near the garage for a few days. Then, I started going for a short drive each day and now feel much better. Still, I'm seriously thinking of trading it in."

"Let me introduce myself. My name is Vincenzo Salini. Cars are my business." He produced a card from his breast pocket and handed it to her.

"I'm Mabel Scattergood." She looked at the card. Not French after all. Vincenzo Salini was definitely an Italian name. "Do you sell sports cars?"

"We specialize in them." He hesitated. "Look, why don't you let me buy you lunch, and we can talk about it? It will give you a clearer idea of what to look for in a sports car."

Mabel gulped. A total stranger was picking her up in the club car park. Oh, dear! About to make an excuse, Mabel saw the club gossip Karla Jackman pull into the driveway.

Karla climbed out of her Lexus and put on a phony smile. "Hello there, Mabel. Long time no see. You're late for lunch as well." Karla's glance shifted from Mabel to Vincenzo, her eyes full of curiosity.

Something about Karla got under Mabel's skin. *You can be sure that she's only stopped to speak to me because she wants to know whom I'm with*, Mabel thought. "Oh, no," she said, "I'm going out for lunch with Vincenzo." Karla's face grew very pink.

Vincenzo seemed to sense what was going on. He introduced himself to Karla. "I'm delighted to meet one of Mabel's friends," he smiled, "but I'm afraid we have to leave, as we will be late for our reservation." He took Mabel by the arm and lowered his voice. "Allow me to drive. We will pick up your car later."

Mabel let him guide her to his Mercedes. He opened the car door for her, and within half a minute, they were driving towards the club's exit. "What reservation?" she finally managed to say. She was beginning to lose her nerve. What had she let herself in for?

"Of course, I don't have a reservation. It was something I thought of on the spur of the moment, but I'm sure that Joseph will find us a table." He smiled. "I think we gave your friend Karla a shock."

Mabel glanced through the window and saw Karla staring after them. Despite her misgivings, she smiled.

"That's better. Now relax. I promise that I will have you back in the car park no later than 2:30."

Vincenzo Salini was wonderful company. His manners were impeccable, and he told her all about the type of sports cars his company sold, recommending several models he felt would suit. Over the avocado soup, Mabel came to a decision. She would go along to his showroom and choose a new car.

Once she'd decided, she felt better and settled back to enjoy herself. It isn't every day that a handsome stranger comes along and whisks you off for lunch, she reasoned, even if he is a foreigner. She intended to make the most of it. Come to think of it, she hadn't really dated anyone since her dear hubby Alf died of a heart attack ten years ago, unless she counted her friend, Bart, who took her for ballroom dancing lessons every Monday evening and to the occasional movie.

As promised, Vincenzo dropped Mabel off at the club by 2:30. He arranged for Mabel to visit the showroom the next afternoon.

The day was bright and sunny, a perfect day to look at cars. A young blonde woman sat at the reception desk, filing her nails. She wore a lime green spandex top, so low cut it left nothing to the imagination.

Mabel walked over to the desk. "Good morning, I have an appointment with Mr. Salini," Mabel noticed the name *GRETA* on the strategically placed nametag.

Sighing irritably, Greta slammed the nail file on the desk. She flicked through a desk calendar. "Your name? I don't see anyone booked for 10:00."

Mabel felt her hackles rise. *People like Greta give blondes a bad name.* "Mabel Scattergood. I'm a few minutes early."

Greta didn't move for a few moments. She cleared her throat and turned to Mabel, smiling. "Mrs. Scattergood, welcome to Salini's. My boss is expecting you. He'll be along shortly. Would you like a coffee or tea while you wait?"

Mabel found Greta's sudden change of attitude amusing. She might as well enjoy the VIP treatment. "Tea, please, with a drop of milk."

Vincenzo arrived just as she finished her tea, and for the next hour, he escorted her as she examined a range of upscale sports cars. She sat in a white Ferrari, admired a hunter green Maserati, and received all kinds of statistics on the showroom models.

"Do you stock other makes? These are beautiful cars, but they're much too expensive."

"Do not worry," Vincenzo assured her. "I'm expecting a new shipment tomorrow. We will find you a car that makes your heart sing."

***

Two days later, Vincenzo invited Mabel to the dealership and showed her a white Lotus Elise with black leather upholstery and a leather steering wheel cover. Vincenzo told her the cost of the car, and it was well within her price range. She climbed into the car and sank into the well-padded seat.

"Now, we'll take it for a test drive," Vincenzo declared.

They drove into the country along winding roads, where Mabel had many opportunities to test the gear changes, the car's acceleration, and the engine's power. By the time they got back to the showroom, she'd made up her mind. "I've found the car I want," she told Vincenzo. "Except for the colour. I'd like a red one."

"That is no problem."

"Good."

"I am delighted to be of help," he said. "Now, I need to take down the necessary details, so I can prepare the paperwork. In the meantime, let us celebrate your new purchase. We will dine at Il Carpaccio, the best Italian ristorante in Toronto."

Mabel's stomach clenched. "Dinner?"

"Yes, I will pick you up at 7:00."

Mabel's mind raced. Here she was, invited out to a fancy restaurant, and she had nothing suitable to wear. Crammed into her messy wardrobe were bright floral dresses, stretch knit pants, and tops in neon green, pink, and canary yellow. And she didn't even own a pair of dressy high-heeled shoes. She mumbled something about a prior arrangement.

"I understand. It is very short notice."

Mabel breathed an inward sigh of relief.

"We will go tomorrow evening instead. That is, if you are free."

"I—yes, I am."

He smiled. "Drive carefully, Mabel. I will pick you up tomorrow at 7:00."

It wasn't until she was close to home that reality sank in. She'd have to buy a new outfit. As clothes didn't interest her, she purchased most of her clothing at discount outlets and chose more for price than style. She thought how elegant Dottie always looked. If they hadn't had that stupid quarrel, she could have asked Dottie to help her. It was time to patch up their differences. She would phone Dottie when she got home.

As Mabel pulled into the driveway, a thought struck her. If she told Dottie about Vincenzo, she would lecture her about picking up strange men in parking lots and give all kinds of advice. No, she would shop by herself. What was the name of that posh place in Toronto where Dottie always shopped? Holt Renfrew. She would go there.

***

Who knew that personal shoppers could be so helpful? By the time Mabel walked out of Holt Renfrew, she felt very pleased with herself. What if the neckline plunged too much and the lip-gloss made her lips shine a deep rusty colour? It was time she lived it up a little.

When she arrived home and plopped down with exhaustion into the nearest chair, the full impact of what she'd done sank in. What madness possessed her to spend all that money? It wasn't as if she was being flown to Paris for the weekend or about to embark on a passionate affair. She'd been invited out for dinner. She tried on the dress again with the sexy gold sandals. The new Mabel stared back at her in the full-length mirror. "Well, Mabel Scattergood, you're looking pretty good," she said aloud. "All you need is a different hairstyle and a good body-shaping undergarment, and you'll do very nicely."

***

She allowed plenty of time to get ready for her dinner date with Vincenzo. In her jewelry box, she found a string of pearls with matching earrings. Too ordinary, she decided, and opted for a gold pendant and earrings, which would complement the green silk dress. She must try to keep her mind off the body-shaping garment gripping her like a vice and concentrate on the evening ahead. She could hardly see anything without glasses but was determined not to spoil her new look by wearing those winged ones. She would put them in her purse, just in case she needed them. She glanced at her watch. For once in her life, she was early—fifteen minutes, to be precise.

She paced the room in her new shoes but soon discarded them. No point in starting the evening with sore feet. When 7:00 came and went, and 7:15 rolled around, Mabel had convinced herself that Vincenzo was not going to show up.

He arrived at 7:20. Full of apologies, he took her by the hand. "You look very glamorous!"

"Thank you." Mabel felt herself blush. No man had ever described her that way. She'd been called sensible, high-spirited, and a good sport. Her hubby Alf – God rest his soul!– called her his little woman. Once, when she was a teenager, she had even been called pretty by a young man whose eyesight was questionable. But "glamorous" spoke of glitzy nightclubs and expensive champagne.

"I must get my evening bag. Come in for a moment." Vincenzo followed Mabel into the living room while she ran upstairs for the bag.

When she returned, Mabel found Vincenzo studying a landscape oil painting. "A fine painting," he remarked.

Mabel frowned. "Do you think so? I've always found it to be rather dull."

"You have more oil paintings?"

"Quite a few. They've been in our family for generations."

"Is that so?"

She sighed. "To be truthful, I'm not keen on them. I prefer bright cheerful paintings."

"Have you thought about selling them?"

"It has crossed my mind."

"I might be able to help you. Leave it with me." He smiled. "At this moment, let us go out for dinner and enjoy ourselves." He placed her hand in the crook of his arm. "May I have the pleasure of escorting you to the car?"

As he ushered her into the passenger seat, his cell phone rang. Apologising for the interruption, Vincenzo walked away from the car, cell phone to his ear. A minute into the call, Mabel heard his raised voice, but couldn't make out the words. *Oh, dear,* she thought, *the call's obviously upsetting him. I wonder if he's going to cancel our dinner.*

Five minutes later, he returned to the car. Frowning, he climbed into the driver's seat and turned on the ignition.

She stole a glance at him as he drove along the Queen Elizabeth Highway into the city. In his navy blazer, dark hair greying at the temples, he looked magnificent. A man who had everything. So why did he grip the steering wheel so tightly that his knuckles turned white? In a car's passing headlights, she noticed a band of sweat on his forehead. He's still upset over that phone call, she decided.

***

When they were seated, Mabel knew she was in trouble. The garter stuck into her legs, and as she bent down to retrieve the linen napkin that had slipped off her lap, the body armour pushed into her rib cage. She heard the waiter's voice. "To begin the meal, I recommend Carpaccio di Manzo."

Mabel straightened up to find Vincenzo and the waiter looking at her. "That sounds wonderful," she said, not having any idea what she'd ordered. She chose gnocchi with vodka sauce for the main course.

Vincenzo ordered a bottle of Chianti. He tasted the wine, rolling the liquid around his tongue before giving a discreet nod. With a white napkin wrapped around the bottle, the waiter poured them each a glass.

When the waiter was out of earshot, Vincenzo raised his glass. "To your health and happiness, Mabel." He smiled. "This will be an evening to remember. Our first dinner together." He put down his glass. "Have you ever been to France?"

"I spent a week in Paris with my husband about twenty years ago."

"My favourite area is Provence." The stress he'd been under when he took that phone call seemed to fade away as he described the lavender fields, the hilltop villages, and the vineyards. By the time he'd finished, Mabel decided that was where she'd spend her next vacation.

"It sounds wonderful."

As if reading her thoughts, he said, "I can see you dashing around France in a fancy sports car."

"So can I. My friend Dottie won't believe I've bought a new car. She's been nagging me for months to get rid of my Porsche."

Vincenzo began to cough. "Excuse me," he managed to say between sips of water.

"Are you all right?"

He dabbed his eyes. "Yes, thank you. A little tickle in my throat..."

The waiter brought the first course. She looked at the thin slices of red meat garnished with shaved parmesan cheese and mushrooms. "What's this?"

Vincenzo laughed. "It's Carpaccio, the house specialty. I promise you will like it."

"It's raw meat!"

Never in her life had Mabel eaten raw flesh. Her mother always cooked meat until it was crispy black on the outside, and Mabel had continued that tradition. Still, this was no time to be squeamish. She took a large mouthful of wine before forking a small piece of beef into her mouth. By swallowing some wine first, she managed to eat most of it. If it weren't for the fact that she knew the meat was raw, she would have enjoyed it, for it had a delicious flavour.

When the waiter placed the main entrée in front of her, Mabel breathed in the aroma of basil sprinkled over the sauce. "This smells wonderful."

Vincenzo looked pleased. "I'm very happy that you think so. The lamb racks are cooked to perfection, as always, so I too am pleased with my choice." He cut into the lamb. "You started to tell me about your friend Dottie."

"That's right. Dottie wanted me to get rid of the car. She thought it was unsafe. I didn't think so, until the accident." Mabel sighed. "The trouble is we've fallen out. We haven't spoken for weeks now."

Vincenzo looked sympathetic. "I'm sure you will be friends again soon."

"I hope so."

They ate in comfortable silence. Then, halfway through their dessert, Vincenzo's cell phone rang. He frowned. "Excuse me, Mabel, I will be right back."

Five minutes later, he returned. Two pink spots had appeared on his cheeks. He ordered two cappuccinos. "And the bill, please," he snapped. He rubbed his hands over his face. "I am sorry I have to cut short our dinner, Mabel. Something has come up..."

"Think nothing of it; I've had a lovely evening," Mabel assured him.

She tried to make conversation on the drive home, but Vincenzo's responses were monosyllabic. She hoped, for his sake, that he sorted his business problems out soon. Right now, she just wanted to go home, slip into her comfortable old dressing gown, and make herself a pot of tea.

CHAPTER 12

Mabel walked through the front door and kicked off her shoes. Within minutes, she had discarded the dress, corset, and stockings and pulled on her faded bathrobe. That felt so much better. She put on the kettle and set out a cup and saucer. Once the kettle began to whistle, she measured several teaspoons of loose tea into the pot and poured boiling water over it, priding herself on not succumbing to teabags. Settling on the sofa, she flicked through the latest copy of the *National Inquirer* and sipped her tea. Mabel felt naughty as she read its outrageous headlines, and she was engrossed in a story about a UFO when the doorbell rang. It was well past 11 o'clock. Who would be calling at this hour? Pulling the robe tightly around her, she left the safety chain on the door and peered out.

Vincenzo stood in the full glare of the security light, blood streaming from a cut beneath his eye. "Oh, my! What happened to you?" Mabel cried and slipped the safety chain off the hook. She took him by the arm and led him into the living room.

His face was ashen. Brandy was the thing for shock. Mabel rooted in her dining room cabinet and found a dusty bottle of cognac. She poured a healthy measure into a glass and handed it to Vincenzo. He took a couple of sips. "Thank you."

"Finish the drink. I'll get the first-aid kit." Thankful she'd recently completed a first-aid course with the Red Cross, Mabel dabbed the cut with mild soap and water. Stitches wouldn't be necessary, as it wasn't very deep. She applied antibacterial ointment and a plaster.

"You'll do." She looked at him. "You still haven't told me what happened."

Vincenzo's eyes darted away from hers. "It was… someone attacked me."

"Where? We must call the police."

Vincenzo's eyes grew wide in alarm. "No, no, there's no need. It was just a… misunderstanding." Although the wound wasn't serious, Vincenzo seemed a bit dazed. He shouldn't be driving; he would have to stay the night. She didn't relish the idea, as she didn't have the spare bed made up. Still, it wouldn't take long to make the bed. She rooted in her linen closet for sheets and pillowcases, but by the time she returned to the living room, he'd fallen asleep on the sofa. He looked so comfortable lying there; she decided to leave him. Covering him with a blanket, she switched off the light and closed the door.

***

The early morning sun poured through Mabel's bedroom window. She stretched and yawned. Halfway through the yawn, she remembered Vincenzo. *Had he slept well,* she wondered. Pulling on her dressing gown and slippers, Mabel crept downstairs. When she entered the living room, she found the blanket folded neatly at the foot of the sofa. There was no sign of her overnight guest. She rushed to the window and saw his car was gone. He must have left during the night. She was such a heavy sleeper she didn't hear a thing. Darn it! She'd been looking forward to finding out what had happened to him.

A few minutes later, the phone rang. "It's Vincenzo. May I come over for a few minutes? I have a surprise for you."

"You sound very cheerful. What time did you leave last night?"

"About two."

"I see."

"So, may I come over?"

"Of course. I'll make some coffee for you." Mabel rarely drank the stuff but knew Vincenzo didn't like tea.

The doorbell chimed as she set out mugs and sugar cookies on a tray. Vincenzo stood on the doorstep, a smile playing on his lips. Apart from the plaster beneath his eye, his face showed little sign of the attack, except for some bruising around the nose and jaw. "Are you feeling OK?"

"Yes." He cleared his throat. "Thank you for your help last night, Mabel. I feel much better this morning." He smiled at her. "Before we have coffee, let me show you something." He took her by the arm to guide her outside.

The Lotus Elise sat on the driveway, its glossy red paint glinting in the sunlight. Mabel's heart skipped a beat. "It's gorgeous. I didn't expect delivery for at least a week." She felt an urge to give Vincenzo a hug but thought better of it.

"A colleague of mine has a red one in stock. Why don't we have our drinks, and I'll answer any questions you have about your new car."

She poured coffee for Vincenzo and tea for herself. As they chatted about the car, it struck Mabel as odd that Vincenzo didn't mention last night's attack. He'd landed on her doorstep at close to midnight, the victim of some kind of altercation. She'd cleaned him up and left him sleeping on the sofa, and he hadn't said a word about it. Perhaps he was embarrassed. It was probably a male ego thing. *Best to let it go*, she thought. *For now.*

Mabel itched to take her new car out for a drive. Once they'd finished discussing the car's features, she drove Vincenzo back to the dealership. She checked her watch. Her favourite soap didn't begin until noon, so she had plenty of time to spare. She replaced her purple-winged glasses with a pair of Ray-Ban sunglasses, glanced around to make sure the road was clear, and eased out into the traffic. All worries about Vincenzo vanished as she delighted in the joy of driving through winding country lanes, changing gears, and revving the engine. Few people were around, so she didn't have to worry about traffic or noise pollution.

After an exhilarating drive, Mabel decided to celebrate in style, so she picked up half a dozen Boston creams from Tim Horton's coffee shop. She'd make a pot of Earl Grey tea and treat herself to one of the delicious cream-filled donuts. She pulled into the driveway.

An envelope poked out of the mailbox. She opened the envelope and found a note from Vincenzo.

Dear Mabel,

What a pleasure it was to see your eyes light up when you saw the car. Imagine the thrill of driving it along country lanes, without a care in the earth! I would like to meet you for lunch tomorrow around noon if you are free. I have something to discuss with you. I will give you a phone tonight.

Vincenzo

Mabel smiled as she read the note. His grammatical mistakes were so charming! Still, she was curious. Now that the car purchase was complete, what could Vincenzo possibly want to discuss with her?

***

The doorbell rang at 11:55. Dressed in a light blue wool sweater and charcoal slacks, Vincenzo looked very boyish. "Do you like Indian food? There's a good restaurant just a couple of blocks from here."

"Yes, in fact, I do." Curry Haven, one of Dottie's favourite restaurants, specialized in vegetarian dishes. She and Mabel had eaten there many times.

They ordered the special, curried eggplant. Vincenzo ordered a light beer, but Mabel stuck with mineral water. Once the drinks were served, he turned to Mabel. "You are wondering why I invited you out for lunch." It was more of a statement than a question. "I will not beat around the tree."

"Bush," Mabel said and took a sip of water.

"What? Oh, yes! I get my expressions mixed up sometimes." His eyes crinkled with amusement. "It is a good thing I have you to correct me. Now, where was I?"

At that moment, the waiter arrived with steaming dishes of eggplant and rice. "You were about to tell me something, I think," Mabel said, as she dolloped chutney on her plate.

"Yes." He leaned towards her. "I have a proposition for you. It has to do with the oil painting in your living room."

"That drab landscape?"

"I have a friend in the art business. He is very reliable and has an excellent reputation. He will appraise it for you, if you like."

"You think it's valuable?"

"I believe it is. Would you like to find out?"

"My great uncle left it to me, but it's hard to believe he owned anything of value." She paused. "Yes, I would like to know."

Free of the body shaper and tight shoes she'd worn last night, Mabel ate her meal with enthusiasm. "Does your friend also do jewelry appraisals?" she asked, between mouthfuls of eggplant. "I have an antique gold bracelet set in rubies another aunt left me more than two years ago with some other baubles."

Vincenzo developed a coughing fit. Mabel handed him a glass of water. "You really ought to see a doctor about that cough."

Vincenzo drank the water. "Thank you for your concern, Mabel. It is nothing." He looked at her. "It didn't occur to me to ask you if you had any jewelry. I do know a very good jewelry appraiser. You should have it appraised as soon as possible so that you can get it insured. I will contact him tonight."

"You know an art dealer **and** a jewelry appraiser?"

"I have... diverse business interests." He took a last bite of curry. "Your jewelry is in a safe place, I hope, Mabel. Robbery is quite commonplace, and all kinds of scams are going on."

If he only knew! Her jewelry was in an old box she kept under her bed. When she got home, she would find a better hiding place. After all, her neighbour was robbed just last week. Someone broke into her home while she was at a friend's house playing bridge. *Vincenzo is right*, she thought. *You never know whom you can trust these days.*

***

Vincenzo phoned the next morning at breakfast time. "There is a slight hitch," he told her. "This friend of mine, Antonio, the jewelry appraiser I told you about, is on his way to Amsterdam this evening, and he won't be back for six weeks. And he will be occupied all day in a business meeting."

"Oh, dear." Mabel was disappointed. She'd looked forward to finding out how much her jewelry was worth. "Well, thanks for trying. I can always take it to someone else. I'm sure there are plenty of well-respected appraisers in the city."

"Oh, but it's not as simple as that!" Vincenzo broke in. "Many people are unscrupulous." He paused. "I have an idea. I will phone you back in a few minutes."

Mabel poured out some cereal. By the time she'd eaten half of it, the phone rang again. It was Vincenzo again. "I've just been in touch with Antonio. He will be happy to look at your jewelry before he leaves on his trip."

"I thought he was going to be in a meeting all day."

"Oh, that." Vincenzo cleared his throat. "He will arrange to leave the meeting a little earlier."

"What time should we be at the airport? I have an appointment at two, but I suppose I could cancel that."

"That is the problem. He doesn't know when he can get away. It might be 1 o'clock, but it could be much later." He paused. "I would be happy to take the jewelry myself. That way, you will not miss your appointment."

Mabel was secretly pleased. She hated missing her weekly bridge game.

"If you're sure you don't mind."

"I am delighted to be of assistance. I will come around to your house in an hour to pick it up."

***

As Mabel wrapped each piece of jewelry in soft tissue paper, she thought about her Aunt Augustine. Uncle Cecil had always brought Augustine a new bauble whenever he travelled abroad, and she'd always looked forward to opening her gift.

Mabel broke out in a cold sweat. What if the jewelry appraiser was a thief?

By the time Vincenzo arrived, Mabel had convinced herself that the appraiser was a high-flying Mafia type who smuggled diamonds and heroin for a living. She felt a warm hand on hers. "Mabel, are you all right?"

"Yes. No, I'm not all right." She confronted Vincenzo. "What do you know about this friend of yours, Antonio? How do you know you can trust him?"

Vincenzo produced a gold embossed business card from his wallet. He handed it to Mabel. "I should have given this card to you earlier."

Mabel examined the card closely. "Antonio Minneli, gemstone expert. Specializing in diamonds and rubies." Impressive-looking letters followed his name.

Vincenzo took hold of her shoulders and looked in her eyes. "I wouldn't allow anyone near your jewelry unless I had complete faith. You mean too much to me."

Mabel felt her face heat up. "Well…" She looked again at the card.

"I would not dream of upsetting you," Vincenzo said. "If you do not feel comfortable, we will forget about it."

"Forget about it?"

"Yes."

'What about the painting?"

"The painting. Ah, yes. I will try to get in touch with… my contact this week."

Mabel drew away from Vincenzo and walked over to the coffee table where the jewelry bag lay. She picked it up and handed it to Vincenzo.

He frowned. "You are sure about this?"

"Yes."

A smile spread across his face. "Dear Mabel, I am so happy you are going ahead." He took the bag out of her outstretched hands and strode to the front door. "I will phone you when I have the results of the appraisal." The door slammed shut.

Why had Vincenzo been in such a hurry? Mabel wondered. He'd rushed off without waving or saying goodbye. Her earlier misgivings returned. *If something seems too good to be true, it probably is.* She'd convinced herself that the appraiser was a criminal, but this time, her suspicions turned to Vincenzo. Now that he had her jewelry, would she ever see him again, or had she become the victim of a con artist?

She walked into the kitchen and opened the brown paper bag on the counter. Removing a donut, Mabel closed her eyes and bit into a gooey, chocolate-iced Boston cream. Maybe Vincenzo was on the level, maybe not. She would just have to wait and see, but right now, she wasn't going to think about it. She took another delicious bite of the Boston cream.

***

The next two days were filled with her volunteer work at the hospital, a coffee morning fundraiser for needy families, and a bridge tournament. Keeping busy kept her mind off Vincenzo. By the evening of the third day, Mabel was convinced that she would never set eyes on him—or her jewelry—again. He was probably in the South of France or some such place by now. She glanced at the bottle of cognac on the sideboard that she'd opened for him just a few days ago and poured herself a generous measure. Its strong fumes made her eyes sting. How could she have been so gullible? It was just as well that she and Dottie were not on speaking terms. She could hear Dottie now. "What were you doing, allowing yourself to be taken in like that?" But as Mabel sipped the potent drink, she knew she would have given anything to hear Dottie's voice.

When the phone rang, Mabel grabbed the receiver. "Hello, Dottie!"

"Good evening, Mabel. May I drop over to see you?"

"Vincenzo!"

"I have some good news for you. I'll pick up a bottle of champagne on the way, and we can celebrate."

"Of course," she managed to say. "Come right over."

As she hung up the phone, Mabel's head was spinning. So, she was wrong after all. He didn't take off somewhere. As she searched for champagne glasses and put out some mixed nuts, something came over her. It was the realization that she really didn't care that it had taken him three days to get in touch. She was enjoying the attention of a sophisticated and charming European who knew how to treat a woman. What if he was a bit of a rogue? Smiling to herself, she poured her glass of brandy down the sink, squirted on her new perfume, and gussied up her hair. By the time the doorbell rang, Mabel was in the mood to celebrate.

Vincenzo insisted that they open the champagne right away. With a great flourish, he poured two glasses and handed one to Mabel. "I must congratulate you, Mabel." He took the bag from his jacket pocket and handed it to her. "Here is your jewelry." He smiled. "It's worth quite a large sum of money. I have the appraisal and will go over it with you later, but right now, I have something for you."

Vincenzo produced a velvet box from his pocket and placed it in Mabel's hand.

Curious, Mabel opened the box. Inside was an opal pendant on a silver chain. "It's beautiful! But why are you giving me this?"

He smiled mischievously. "I happen to know that tomorrow is your birthday."

"How did you find out?"

"While I waited for you to get your evening bag the other night, I noticed some cards lying on the coffee table. I am afraid that I couldn't resist looking inside. One card said something like 'have a wonderful day on the 7th.'" He raised his glass. "A very happy birthday to you, Mabel. Now, let us relax and celebrate your good fortune."

Mabel watched Vincenzo as they sipped their champagne. There was something about him that she couldn't pinpoint. To outward appearances, he was the same Vincenzo. Dressed in a brown suede jacket with black slacks, he looked as dashing as ever. Yet, quite apart from the plaster and the bruising, there was pallor to his skin and deep creases around his eyes.

"Is everything all right, Vincenzo? " She stumbled over her words. "You look peaky."

"What is 'peaky'?"

"You look stressed out."

He shot a worried look at her, and then glanced away.

"We can go over the appraisal another time," Mabel suggested. "I'll go through it myself if you like. If I have any questions, I'll get in touch with you."

He ran his fingers through his hair and stifled a yawn. "All right, you can contact me at work."

Mabel was tempted to add that she didn't have any choice in the matter as he hadn't given her his home number but thought better of it. She waved to Vincenzo as he drove off and closed the front door. She bit her lip. She must be patient. If she pushed too hard, he wouldn't disclose anything.

***

As she turned towards the kitchen, Mabel caught her reflection in the hall mirror. The light over the mirror was very bright and showed every wrinkle and blemish, but Mabel didn't need a mirror to tell her that she had too many bulges and too many chins. *No more excuses*, she thought, *it is time for action.* Tomorrow, she would sign up at the Y for a fitness assessment and join Weight Watchers.

CHAPTER 13

Dottie climbed off the stationary bicycle and mopped her face with a hand towel. It felt good to be back in her exercise routine at the Y after four weeks of runny noses, scraped knees, and a puppy that wasn't house-trained. She headed towards the showers. As she turned the corner, a blonde woman in a bright orange tracksuit, eyes glued on a Y pamphlet, careened right into her.

"I'm so sorry..." The woman looked up. Dottie recognized the purple-winged glasses. "Mabel!"

"Dottie! Oh, dear, I wasn't looking..."

"What are you doing here?"

"I'm not really sure." Mabel looked a bit frazzled. "Would you like a cup of coffee? I'm in need of a caffeine fix."

"Since when did you start to drink coffee?"

Mabel smiled weakly. "Since I signed up for a fitness program two minutes ago."

***

The cafe was crowded with women. Dottie ordered two coffees. "Let's sit over there." She pointed to an empty table. They sat down. Mabel poured skimmed milk into her coffee and picked up a packet of sugar. She began tearing the packet open but put it down quickly, giving Dottie a sheepish look. "I'd better start my fitness program off on the right foot." She stirred in the milk. "You know, it's been more than two months since the accident."

"I know," Dottie said.

"I'm glad I bumped into you today," Mabel said in a shaky voice. "I've missed you."

A lump came into Dottie's throat. "And I've missed you. It's been much too long."

Mabel blew her nose. "So, tell me what you've been doing."

"I've just spent four busy weeks at Hettie's." Dottie gave a brief summary of what happened. "Give me my real estate work any day over spoiled grandchildren and a yapping puppy."

"It sounds like a nightmare."

Dottie sipped her coffee. "When I got back from Hettie's yesterday, I drove over to the college and registered for a course."

"In what?"

"Motorbike lessons. They teach you in the parking lot at weekends."

"Motorbike lessons! Whatever for?"

"You know I've always liked bikes, especially Harley-Davidsons. When I lived in Montreal, I often drove them on weekends. That was several years ago. I need to upgrade my skills."

"But you don't have a bike," Mabel pointed out. "Still, you could always rent one."

Dottie fiddled with a plastic stirrer. Should she tell Mabel about Enrique's gift? It needed a bit of explaining. Maybe later.

"I'm glad for your sake that you've taken the plunge, Dottie, if you don't expect me to be a passenger. You wouldn't get me on one of those in a million years." Mabel smiled. "I've got some news as well. I've sold my old car and traded it in for a new one. I finally realized that it was about time I treated myself to another one." She paused for a moment. "You were right, Dottie. I should have done it ages ago. I was being stubborn about it. Just a minute." She reached for her purse. "I have a picture of it in here somewhere."

As Mabel searched, her pendant got caught on the catch of the bag. Dottie helped Mabel to free the chain. She scrutinized the opal stone set in silver. "What an attractive pendant!"

Mabel's face grew pink. "It's a birthday gift." She cleared her throat, "From Vincenzo."

"Vincenzo?"

Mabel kept her eyes focused on the contents of the purse. "He's Italian." She pulled out a picture. "Here it is!" She handed it to Dottie. "I picked up the car a week ago. It's a dream to drive."

Dottie looked at the bright red Lotus Elise in the picture. Without looking up, she asked, "And what does Vincenzo think about the car?"

"He is very enthusiastic about it. In fact," Mabel leaned towards Dottie, "he sold it to me!"

"Aha!"

Mabel sat up straight. "What do you mean, 'aha'?"

"Nothing. It looks very appealing. The most important thing is that you're happy with it."

As they sipped their coffee, Dottie's silver bracelet clinked against her mug.

"Is that new?" Mabel asked, pointing to the bracelet. "I haven't seen you wear it before."

Dottie put down her coffee mug. "It's a gift from Enrique."

Now, it was Mabel's turn to look surprised. "Who's Enrique?"

"A businessman. He is buying an apartment at Queens Quay."

"And you are selling it to him, I presume?"

"Yes, someone had given him my name, so he dropped by to see me." She paused. "The bracelet was to thank me for helping him find an apartment. His niece is going to live in it while attending university, and she's very hard to please. He's been searching for the past few months. I'm the third real estate agent he's tried."

"Third time lucky."

"What? Oh, yes." Dottie felt a flush creep over her face.

"Vincenzo has an associate who's an international jewelry appraiser," Mabel said. "He's just examined some jewelry Aunt Augustine left me, and although I haven't looked closely at the figures yet, it looks as if it's worth quite a lot of money."

"Enrique's a jewelry appraiser," Dottie said.

"That's a coincidence."

By the time they'd finished their coffee, most clients in the cafe had left. "I'm selling tickets for our hospital's annual dinner and dance in two weeks' time," Mabel said. "Why don't I get tickets for the four of us? They have some good raffles. The grand prize this year is a weekend for two in Paris."

Dottie shook her head. "I don't think so."

"It's just a bit of fun. I thought you liked dancing. It's a black-tie event, so we can all dress up to the nines. And the dinner is being catered by a top chef."

"I've been out for dinner with Enrique a few times, and we've become friends. I'm not sure how he'd feel about going to a dinner dance with another couple."

Mabel realized that Vincenzo might have the same reservations. "You might be right. Still, I'm going to do my best to persuade Vincenzo to come with me. It's for a good cause, after all."

Dottie pulled on her jacket. "I really must go, Mabel. I'll call you tomorrow." She paused. "Fancy going to see a movie this week? *Mamma Mia* is on, and it's supposed to be very good."

Mabel's eyes lit up. "I'll look forward to that."

CHAPTER 14

D ottie felt relieved that Mabel hadn't mentioned the
emeralds. It would have been very difficult to explain
why they were still hidden behind the dresser. She'd
intended to hand them in to the police when she returned
from the spa weekend, but then she'd met Enrique and
forgotten about them. That's what she told herself, but who
was she trying to kid? It was time she faced this phobia she
had about the police.

Of course, if George Fernandes hadn't stuffed the
package in her coat pocket, the phobia wouldn't have been
an issue. A chill went down her spine as she remembered
staring at George's inert body on the floor of the casino, a
knife in his back. Was she in danger of meeting the same
fate? She blew out a long breath. By the time she turned
down Baker Lane, she had made up her mind. She'd get in
touch with the police first thing in the morning.

Pulling into the driveway, she remembered the
Sanctuary spa appointment and smiled. She'd have some
cottage cheese for lunch, and then head for the half-day
spa treatment special. As she climbed out of the car, her
smile faded. Her bungalow's front door was wide open. She
ran over to the house. Shards of glass from the door panels
lay on the doorstep. Sidestepping the glass, she ran inside,
straight into her bedroom.

Sweaters, blouses, suits, and dresses, still on their
hangers, were strewn over the floor. Various items of
underwear hung out of opened dressing table drawers. Her
jewelry box was turned upside down, its contents glinting in
the shaft of sunlight that streamed through the blinds. The
bed had been stripped down to the mattress, and bedclothes

were heaped in a pile beside the bed. Even a loose floorboard in the corner of the room had been removed. The two pictures that hung behind her bed lay on the mattress, and several others hung crookedly on the walls.

Dottie removed the wooden backing from the dressing table mirror. The package was still secured to the mirror with tape. Breathing a sigh of relief, she managed a weak smile. Despite a thorough search, the thieves had missed the hiding place. The jewelry was safe—for the time being, anyway.

She was about to phone the police when a piece of folded notepaper caught her eye. It lay beneath a crystal perfume bottle on the dressing table. Fingers trembling, she picked it up. A skull and crossbones insignia was printed in the top right-hand corner. Where had she seen that insignia before? She opened up the paper. The typed message read, "Bring the emeralds to Chicken Licken at Fairweather Mall at 7:00 p.m. Wednesday night and ask for Charlie. We have your cat."

Dottie swallowed hard. Someone was playing a sick joke. Certain that she'd find Muggins asleep in one of his favourite hiding places, Dottie called out his name and dashed around the bungalow, peering under beds, behind sofas, and inside closets.

After the frantic search, Dottie sank into a chair. She felt the blood drain out of her face. Someone had taken Muggins. Whoever had written this note meant business. The threat was clear—do as I say, or your cat will be killed. As far as she could tell, she had no choice in the matter. Yet, if she did as she was instructed, would she end up dead like George? And how did they know she still had the emeralds?

Calling the police would involve answering too many awkward questions. But what should she do? She must ask Mabel's advice. Mabel's phone rang five times, reminding Dottie that Mabel was scheduled to work in the hospital gift shop all afternoon. An idea struck her. Enrique would know what to do. She had misgivings about him, to be sure, but he was a man of the world and should be able to give her sound advice. The more she thought about it, the more the idea appealed to her. The truth was she was frightened and didn't know whom else to turn to. She punched his office number. He wasn't there, so she left a message on his answering machine asking him to call her as quickly as possible. She prayed it would be soon.

She arranged for a local glass and mirror company to fix the door. While she waited for them to arrive, Dottie removed the broken glass and put things back in place. By the time she'd finished, her body ached, and she could feel her temples throb, the early sign of a migraine. A cup of herbal tea might help, she decided, and was about to put on the kettle when the phone rang. It was Enrique.

"Can you come over right away?"

"Dottie, my dear, you sound upset. I hope it is not bad news."

"I can't tell you on the phone."

"Don't worry. I will be right over."

***

Enrique said very little at first. It wasn't until Dottie showed him the threatening note that he showed any emotion. His face grew pale. "It cannot be!" Enrique paced the room.

"What's the matter?"

He turned to her. "These people are dangerous. The skull and crossbones are the trademark of the Skinner gang. They are ruthless, and they will stop at nothing to get what they want."

"At the moment, they want me," Dottie gulped.

"It is not you they want, Dottie; it is the jewelry." He sat down on the sofa next to her.

Despite her anxiety, Dottie was curious. "How do you know about the Skinner gang?"

"I have… contacts. In my business, it pays to know who your enemies are."

Dottie, still puzzled, wanted to ask more questions, but she had to deal with more pressing issues. "To think," she sighed, "that I'd planned to take the jewelry to the police tomorrow."

"Do not be too hasty, Dottie," Enrique urged. "Let me think about this."

"If I give the Skinner gang the jewelry, how will I be certain they won't hurt Muggins?"

"They are not interested in the cat. Muggins is just a means to an end."

"So, now what?"

Enrique stood up. "Leave it to me."

"Where are you going?'

"I need to speak with one of my business associates." He smiled. "I will phone you later when I have some news." Frowning, he pointed to the broken door. "I hope you've arranged for someone to fix this."

"I have. They should be here by now."

A man's voice rang out. "Hello! Anyone home?"

"That's probably the glass people."

"I'm glad they are here," Enrique said. "I will feel easy in my mind knowing you are secure again." Enrique touched her hand. "One more thing, Dottie. Do not breathe a word of this to anyone."

In spite of Enrique's assurances, Dottie could see uncertainty in his eyes. Danger lurked, and she had plonked him right in the middle of it.

While the men worked on the door, Dottie mulled over her conversation with Enrique. "The skull and crossbones are the trademark of the Skinner gang," Enrique had said. Now, she remembered a sticker with that insignia had been attached to the ear of the dead cat she'd found under the hydrangea bushes. Had the Skinner gang put the cat in her garden? She remembered how fearful her neighbour Larry had become when she'd told him about the dead cat. Maybe the Skinner gang had intended to put the cat in Larry's garden as some kind of warning but left it in Dottie's garden by mistake. Was Larry mixed up with the Skinner gang?

***

She paced back and forth, chain smoking. It was 7:00 p.m., and she still hadn't heard from Enrique. When the phone rang just after 7:00, she grabbed it with shaking hands. "Hello!" Her voice trembled as she spoke.

"Dottie, it's Mabel. Are you all right? You sound funny."

"It's a long story. Right now, I'm waiting for a phone call."

"From Enrique, I expect."

"Yes."

"I'll leave you to it. Call me later, so we can arrange to see that musical *Mamma Mia*."

"What?"

"Never mind, Dottie. I'll talk to you later."

No sooner had Mabel hung up the phone than it rang again. When Dottie heard Enrique's voice, she almost cried with relief. "Thank God!"

"Listen very carefully to what I have to say, Dottie."

As Enrique outlined his plan, Dottie could feel panic threatening to overcome her. "You're saying that your friend can make copies of the jewelry by Wednesday evening?" Dottie tried to keep a level head. "Even if the thieves are fooled into thinking the jewelry is the genuine article, it won't take them long to find out they've been duped."

"True, but they cannot blame you for that. Many people have copies made of valuable jewelry. They often prefer to put their real jewelry in a safety deposit box and wear their fake jewelry instead. I will get back to you when I can. I have some loose strings to tie up first. And remember, Dottie, if so much a hint of this comes out, it could be very dangerous... for both of us."

When Dottie hung up the phone, she rooted out her long cigarette holder. Even though her hands shook, she managed to insert a cigarillo in the holder, but it took several flicks before she got the lighter to work.

Once she lit the cigarillo, Dottie flopped onto the sofa and inhaled deeply. This whole situation was becoming scarier and scarier—first, George Fernandes, then Billy and Den, now the Skinner gang. By the time she went to bed, Dottie had made up her mind about two things. First, she would take the jewelry to the police once she retrieved Muggins. Second, if the Skinner gang started to bother her, she'd protest her innocence. She would tell them that George Fernandes must have slipped the jewelry into her pocket at the casino. How was she to know they were fake?

As she turned out the light, she shivered. What if the police didn't believe her?

CHAPTER 15

Over the next few days, two big real estate deals kept Dottie occupied, so she had little time to dwell on Enrique. He phoned her on Tuesday morning. "Everything's fixed. I'll bring the jewelry around to your house tomorrow about noon."

"I have bad vibes about this."

"Don't worry, Dottie, you will be taken care of "

"Isn't that another term for doing away with somebody?"

Enrique laughed. "You have been reading too many crime novels, my dear."

"Mabel reads crime novels, not me."

"Trust me, Dottie; no harm will come to you. The main thing right now is to get Muggins back safely."

***

The next day, Enrique dropped off the jewelry. He handed her two large envelopes. "The white envelope contains the jewelry you will give to Charlie at Chicken Licken. The manila envelope contains the real jewelry, which you will take to the police."

Dottie heard the tension in his voice. "Let me get you some coffee."

Enrique glanced at his watch. "I have a few minutes. Coffee would be very welcome." He smiled and patted her hand. "Do not worry about tonight. I will be watching. I will not let anything happen to you."

Dottie wasn't sure if Enrique's attempts at reassuring her helped. What did he think might happen?

Over coffee, Enrique told Dottie things he'd heard about the Skinner gang from a business associate. It was scary stuff. Among other things, they were under police surveillance for suspected drug dealing and several armed robberies. More recently, they were suspected of breaking into houses of wealthy people and stealing paintings and jewelry.

***

Dottie dressed in comfortable slacks, a sweater, and jogging shoes. The shoes might come in handy if she had to make a run for it. Deep breathing exercises and yoga failed to keep her nerves at bay, so she ended up pacing the living room, chain smoking. The fingers of the clock crept by. Finally, it was 6:30. Time to go. Grabbing the envelope from the hallstand, she picked up her car keys and left.

Arriving at the mall fifteen minutes early, Dottie picked up a coffee and found a bench to sit down. She sipped the hot drink. *What would happen tonight,* she wondered. Would she be able to get Muggins back? What if they decided to kidnap her as well? Maybe she should go home and forget about the whole thing, but the thought of poor Muggins, imprisoned in some dingy box, brought her back to reality. At 6:59, she stood up, threw away the empty Styrofoam cup, and walked over to Chicken Licken. Taking a deep breath, she opened the bright red door.

With red plastic tables, sparkling clean tiled floor, and brightly coloured pictures of chicken dinner specials lined up behind the counter, it looked like any other fast food outlet. She had to remind herself that this was no ordinary diner. Somewhere in the back, they had Muggins, who was probably frantic by now.

A teenager with purplish hair and a nose ring stood behind the counter, a bored expression on her face. The bright red uniform, embroidered with Chicken Licken's logo, clashed with the purple hair. "Can I help you?"

Dottie moistened her lips and forced a smile. "I'd like to speak with Charlie."

"I don't know if he's here. He might be 'round the back. I'll go see." The girl turned to leave, and then glanced back over her shoulder. "Who shall I say's looking for him?"

Dottie gave her name. "He's expecting me," she added and immediately regretted her words. They sounded like a line out of a "B" gangster movie.

Within a minute or two, the girl reappeared. Her eyes, full of curiosity, never left Dottie's face. "He says you're to go around to the back of the store."

Dottie thanked her. "How will I know who Charlie is?"

"He knows who you are. He's waiting for you."

Dottie fought back the urge to throw up. Thank God, Enrique was looking out for her. He'd promised to hide nearby and watch just in case.

Dottie walked up to the back entrance of Chicken Licken. The door opened slightly. "In here!" a sharp voice commanded. Dottie glanced around on the off chance she would catch a glimpse of Enrique, but there was no sign of him. Taking a deep breath, she stepped inside. Her eyes took a few seconds to adjust to the dimly lit interior.

"Have you got the jewelry?" a voice asked

Dottie's heart pounded. It would help if she could see the owner of the voice.

"Yes. I have it with me."

"Put it on that table over there, so as I can look."

Dottie was not in the habit of taking orders from anyone, especially from someone who didn't even have the decency to reveal his face. "I'm not giving you the jewelry until I know that Muggins is safe," she retorted, amazed at her audacity. As if on cue, a plaintive meow filled the room. Dottie rushed in the general direction of the cry and found a cardboard box lying on the floor. She could see the white spot on the end of Muggins' nose through a hole at the side of the box. She swallowed hard. Now was not the time for sentiment.

"The jewelry, lady." There was an underlying threat in the tone.

"How do I know you'll give me back my cat?"

"What do I want with a cat?"

Dottie's hand instinctively reached for the pocket where the jewelry lay. "I'm taking Muggins. I'll leave the jewelry on the table." She fully expected the voice to object.

"Go ahead."

Just as Dottie bent down to pick up the cardboard box, the voice growled. "No tricks, mind. I don't take kindly to anyone who tries to cross me."

Dottie withdrew the envelope containing the jewelry from her pocket and placed it on the table. With the cardboard box in her arms, she marched to the door, her heart racing. When she stepped outside, she took several deep gulps of air to calm herself down. She was about to rush away when she spotted Enrique. Peering at her from behind a dumpster, he gave her two thumbs up.

CHAPTER 16

T he next morning, Dottie phoned the police. "I'd like to speak with the officer in charge of the George Fernandes murder case."

For the next half an hour, she was put on hold, questioned, put on hold again, and finally, she got through to a Detective Blake.

"What's your connection with this case?" he demanded in a husky voice.

Taking a deep breath, Dottie proceeded to explain how she and Mabel had been in the casino when George Fernandes was killed and that they were both questioned and released. Detective Blake's voice was polite but firm. "Excuse me, Mrs. Flowers, I appreciate what you're telling me, but why the phone call?"

"When Mabel and I reached the spa where we had booked in for the weekend, I found a package in my jacket." Dottie took another deep breath. "Inside the package were a diamond-and-emerald necklace and a matching set of earrings. George Fernandes must have put them in my jacket pocket just before he was killed."

Detective Blake cleared his throat. In a very official voice, he said, "I think, Mrs. Flowers, you had better come down to the police station and make a statement."

When she hung up the phone, she let out a long breath. This would be a challenge. In her youth, she had been an amateur actress. She would need all her acting skills to make Detective Blake understand why she'd waited this long to get in touch with the police.

After glancing over the chic dresses and figure-hugging skirts in her closet, Dottie realized that her clothing would not portray the right image. Then, she remembered an outfit that had belonged to dear Aunt Agatha. The mauve wool suit with a pleated skirt and box jacket was tucked away in a cedar chest. Dottie had been tempted to give it to charity, but fond memories of her aunt had compelled her to keep it. The suit, with a high-necked blouse with a lace collar and her mother's cameo brooch, would be perfect. At the back of her closet, she found a pair of sturdy lace-up shoes bought for a charity walk. The walk had been cancelled, so the shoes had never been worn. A felt hat with a feather curling at the back of it was discarded. Overkill.

She placed the jewelry inside a well-worn, crocodile-skin handbag she'd found at the bottom of the chest. She put on the clothing and an old pair of spectacles. Fortunately, her prescription hadn't changed much over the years, so she could see quite well out of them. When she looked in the full-length mirror, Dottie hardly recognized the fussy-looking matron staring back at her. The effect was just right.

***

At the police station, Dottie was ushered into a dingy room, where the furniture consisted of a badly scratched table and two wooden chairs. It reminded her of an old Dick Tracy movie set, except for the video camera that blinked in the corner of the room. Her heart raced as memories of the interrogations all those years ago rushed back. She closed her eyes and breathed slowly.

As her heartbeat slowed down, footsteps pounded along the corridor outside the room. The door rattled open. A man wearing a light brown business suit walked in, followed by a woman in police uniform. His youthful appearance belied his stern expression as he shook hands with Dottie and

introduced himself as Detective Blake. He introduced the
woman as Detective Constable Ruth Mayes. He explained
that D.C. Mayes would take notes. "Please sit down, Mrs.
Flowers." He settled in the chair on the opposite side
of the table, opened his briefcase, and pulled out a file
folder. After quickly glancing over the folder's contents, he
explained that the interview would be videotaped. "Are you
ready, Mrs. Flowers?" Dottie nodded. D.C. Mayes switched
on the video camera. As the detective stated the date and
purpose of the interview, deep-seated memories of the
police interview many years ago flooded back. She'd been
under suspicion of embezzlement. After hours of relentless
questions and numerous cups of rank-tasting coffee, she'd
been allowed to go home.

The detective looked at Dottie. "May I have the
jewelry?" As she passed the envelope to him, his hooded
eyes seemed to penetrate through her. "This case is two
months old. Why did it take you until now to hand in the
jewelry?"

Dottie found a tissue in her purse and dabbed her eyes.
"I know I should have brought it to you right away, but
seeing that poor man lying in the casino with a knife stuck
in his back, I was so upset I didn't know what to do."

"What prompted you to bring in the jewelry today. Why
not yesterday or tomorrow?"

"My nerves are worse than ever. I have to take sleeping
pills. I thought that clearing my conscience would help me
to cope."

"Why do you think that George Fernandes put the
package in your pocket?"

"We knew each other slightly in high school. I'd catch
sight of him sometimes at parties, that sort of thing. I met
him again recently on a riding trek through the wineries. In
Niagara."

"A riding trek?" A look of disbelief crossed his face. *He probably can't imagine me on a horse,* Dottie mused. *Or maybe he's wondering what George Fernandes was doing on a winery ride.*

"And you think he recognized you at the casino?"

"Yes."

"Why do you suppose he put the jewelry in your pocket?"

"I think he was being followed. When he saw me, he probably figured that if the jewelry was in my possession, he could retrieve it later."

"Ah! So, you were on friendly terms with George Fernandes?"

"No way!" Dottie decided it was time to tell Detective Blake about the riding fiasco. She embellished it as much as she could to try to convince him how revolting she found George Fernandes. "And with my heart condition, it's all been too much!" she added for good measure. She took out another tissue and blew her nose.

Detective Black switched off the tape recorder. He cleared his throat and spoke in a stern voice. "Mrs. Flowers, you realize that not bringing the jewelry to us right away is an obstruction of justice."

Dottie's hands were folded in her lap and her eyes downcast. "Yes, Detective Blake, I realize that."

"I'm going to let you go with a caution."

Relief rushed through Dottie's veins. "Thank you."

"If you ever find yourself with information that pertains to a crime, make sure that you let the police know right away. You won't get away so lightly next time."

"I will."

Gathering his papers, he returned them to the briefcase with the white envelope containing the jewelry. He headed to the door. "Goodbye, Mrs. Flowers."

"Goodbye, Detective Blake."

After he'd left, Dottie resisted the temptation to hurry away. She must maintain the sedate, middle-aged matron image at least until she was out of the police station.

Driving home, Dottie rehashed the interview. Detective Blake had been fair, if a little intimidating. Whatever possessed her to tell him she had a heart condition? Saying her nerves were bad was one thing, but a heart condition! If her medical records were checked, she could be in deep trouble.

Even though the interview had only taken half an hour, it seemed much longer. Dottie remembered how relieved she'd felt when Detective Blake tucked the white envelope containing the jewelry into his briefcase. Thank goodness, the ordeal was over. She walked into her bungalow. As she glanced at the hallstand where the envelopes had laid, Enrique's words came rushing back. "Give the white envelope to Chicken Licken. The manila envelope contains the real jewelry. Do not mix them up." Her hand shot to her mouth. She had mixed them up!

How could she have been so careless? She'd given Charlie the real jewelry and the police the fake jewelry.

CHAPTER 17

For a few days after the Chicken Licken fiasco, Dottie took time off work. Muggins barely left her side. He watched her every move and followed her around the bungalow, making strange growling noises as he wound himself around her legs. It was a bit cloying, but the poor cat had suffered a terrible trauma. Being cooped up in a cardboard box was enough to drive any animal crazy. By the end of the week, he returned to his old habit of ignoring her, appearing only for food. After eating, he'd purr loudly while Dottie stroked his fur. Then, tail in air, he'd retire to the old couch in the den for a snooze.

By the end of the week, she still hadn't heard from Enrique. The last she'd seen of him was at the shopping mall, hiding behind a dumpster. Although she wondered why he hadn't phoned, she wasn't looking forward to telling him that she'd given Charlie the wrong envelope.

When Mabel suggested a weekend in Toronto, Dottie jumped at the chance to get away. "I'll ask my neighbour Margaret to look after Muggins. They're great friends, and she's always pestering me to take a vacation, so she can have him to herself. I'll tell her to take care he stays inside."

"I'll put Fifi in the kennels." Mabel sounded pleased. "It'll be good to have a break before Yolanda and Arnold arrive. They're coming to stay with me next week. They are so much in love. Who would have believed it? "

Who indeed! Dottie's role in Arnold's pursuit of Yolanda had paid off. "I'm happy for them."

Dottie made reservations at her favourite downtown hotel, the Four Seasons. She had a client who told her any time she wanted Maple Leaf hockey tickets to let him know. He was as good as his word. "And they're gold seats," he assured her. She also managed to pull a few strings to get theatre tickets for *Mamma Mia.* They still hadn't seen the film version, but that could wait.

On Friday night, they sang along with the Abba songs performed in *Mamma Mia*, and at one stage, joined other theatregoers and danced in the aisles. Over a late supper at a small Italian restaurant near the theater, Dottie told Mabel about the kidnapping and rescue of Muggins. "If Enrique hadn't been keeping watch from behind that dumpster, I don't think I would have had the nerve to go through with it."

Pushing negative thoughts about the Skinner Gang to the back of her mind, Dottie tucked into a vegetarian lasagne dish, surprised at how hungry she was. Still, they hadn't eaten since lunchtime. After a few mouthfuls, she glanced at her friend who was gazing into space, the gnocchi with vodka sauce untouched. "Is something wrong, Mabel? You look distracted."

Mabel blinked and looked at Dottie. "When you mentioned Chicken Licken, it struck a chord. Something I read. Oh well, never mind. It'll come back to me."

***

They spent most of Saturday at the Eaton Centre power shopping. They even managed to squeeze in a thirty-minute nap before getting ready for the hockey game. In their Maple Leaf sweatshirts, they left in plenty of time to grab a hot dog and beer before the game. They shouted, cheered, and yelled, and their team won 2–1. After the excitement of the hockey game, they decided to find a quieter spot and grab a light snack.

With the weekend crowds, it wasn't easy, but they managed to find a small bistro near a nightclub on King. A

131

waiter ushered them to a table for two by the window. After ordering some wine and a cheese platter, Dottie breathed a sigh of relief. "I was beginning to think we'd never find a restaurant that wasn't fast food or too upscale."

"This is perfect," Mabel agreed. "We can enjoy our drink and people-watch at the same time."

Dottie sipped a red Shiraz and watched young people sauntering along the street in groups, laughing and shoving one another in play. Theatregoers spilled out of the Princess of Wales and the Royal Alex, some heading for their cars, Dottie supposed others for bars and restaurants. A fight broke out among a group of teens right outside the window. Angry voices filtered into the bistro as one young guy punched another one in the chest. After some jeering and name-calling, the group moved on.

They ordered a second glass of wine. "Why not?" Dottie shrugged. "We aren't going anywhere, and we can take a cab back to the hotel."

By the time they left the bistro, it was getting late. People were already trickling out of clubs and pubs. As they passed by one club, Mabel grabbed Dottie by the arm. "Look over there! That's Billy, I'm sure of it!"

Dottie strained to look where Mabel pointed. In the dim light, the faces of people who stood outside the club, smoking and chatting, were a blur. Just then, headlights from a passing car swept over them, lighting up their faces for a few seconds. Dottie's hand went to her throat when she recognized the scrawny face and prominent scar. "It's Billy, all right."

"Shall we go after him?"

"No way!"

"What do you mean, no way?"

"I don't want to be found lying in a pool of blood somewhere..."

"We might never get a chance like this again," Mabel insisted. "Look at what those two losers, Billy and Den, have put us through!"

Mabel's determination rubbed off on Dottie. "You're right, Mabel. Enough is enough. It's time we showed them just what we are made of." At that moment, Billy started to walk away from the club. "Quick! He's leaving—let's head him off! Thank God, we're wearing sneakers!"

The women ran after him. Shoulders hunched forward, he slouched along, pausing briefly to tie a shoelace. The crowds of people on the sidewalk reassured Dottie. *Safety in numbers*, she thought. It didn't take long to catch up with Billy. They overtook him, turned, and jumped in front of him. His mouth dropped open. As his eyes darted over the two women, a flicker of recognition crossed his face. He tried to run.

"Not so fast, buster!" Mabel shouted, as she and Dottie blocked his way. "You and your buddy Den have some explaining to do." People turned around when they heard the raised voice. Some hurried on, while others stopped to watch.

Without missing a beat, Billy reached into his shirt pocket for a packet of cigarettes and matches. He lit up and took a deep drag. "I dunno know what you mean."

Dottie joined in. "Following us to that spa, then causing us to have an accident. And what about the break-in? You and Den made a terrible mess of my bedroom."

Billy, who was about to take another drag of his cigarette, froze. "I don't know nothin' about no break-in!" He chucked the cigarette into the gutter.

"We need to talk," Dottie said. "Find us a pub."

They followed Billy down a side street into a crowded pub smelling of stale beer and sweat. "I'll get the drinks," said Billy. *He's feeling guilty or scared. Or both,* Dottie thought.

Dottie and Mabel ordered lemonade, while Billy ordered beer. Glasses in hand, they settled in a corner booth, away from the crowds. The two women exchanged glances, and then looked at Billy. "We're waiting," said Mabel.

Billy lit up another cigarette. "Me and Den, we do the odd job here and there," he began, pausing to take several drags of his cigarette.

"Go on," urged Dottie. "We haven't got all night."

Billy looked first at Dottie then at Mabel. He leaned towards them. "Look, it wasn't me and Den who broke into your house." His eyes shifted around the room and landed back on Dottie and Mabel. "Darker forces are at work here," he whispered.

Dottie felt an urge to burst out laughing at Billy's melodramatic words but took a deep swallow of lemonade instead. "Darker forces?"

Again, Billy's eyes shifted around the room before he spoke. "Have you heard of the Skinner gang?"

Dottie felt her heart sink. She turned to Billy. "You'd better tell us all you know."

***

Over another round of drinks, Billy told them the Skinner gang had started out with robberies. "Now, they're into money laundering and all that shit. Anyone tries to cross 'em..." He drew his index finger across his throat. Dottie shuddered. They sounded very like the tales Enrique had told her. "Sometimes, they warn people."

"How?" Mabel asked, her eyes wide open.

"Dead cats." Billy blew out a smoke ring.

134

"Dead cats?"

Dottie tried to keep her voice level. "They leave a dead cat with a skull and crossbones insignia on its fur close by, maybe in the garden, so the person gets the message and backs off."

Billy looked puzzled. "How d'you know that?"

"Let's just say I have my sources," Dottie said.

"Their leader's name is Rocco," Billy continued. Dottie could see the whites of his eyes. He took several gulps of beer, and then wiped his hand across his mouth. "They've been after me and Den. Following us around, eh. They think we got the jewelry. Den and me—we thought you got it." He looked at Dottie. "We didn't mean you no harm. We only do small jobs, TVs, cameras, stuff like that. It was George Fernandes who got us into this mess."

"George Fernandes?"

"He overheard them talking about this break-in. The house is in the sticks. About ten miles from the casino. The owners are a coupla rich Brazilians."

"How did they—the Skinner gang—find out about the jewelry?"

"The housekeeper. She's Snake's sister."

"Who's Snake?"

"He's one of Rocco's boys. George got word of the break-in and decided to beat them to it. He promised me and Den a tidy share in the profits. It was easy money, he said. After the job was done, we was to meet up with George at the casino. I wasn't keen, but George said an hour at the casino wouldn't do no harm."

"So, you think a member of the Skinner Gang killed George?"

Billy swallowed a mouthful of beer. "Yeah, my guess it was Snake. We—me and Den—saw him hanging around the casino."

"Why did the gang want George out of the way?"

"The robbery really pissed them off." He caught Dottie's eye. "Pardon my French. No one crosses the Skinner gang and gets away with it."

"Why didn't they go after you?" Mabel asked.

"They didn't know we was connected with George. When we got to the casino, we spotted Snake followin' 'im. We knew something was up. We tried to stay close, but when you won the jackpot, it got confusing. When things got quiet, we saw what happened to George, and we got out fast."

So, it **was** Den and Billy that Dottie saw running out of the casino. "They found out about your connection with George later?"

Billy nodded. His face had grown pale, and his hands shook as he took a last swig from the glass.

"You haven't explained why you were chasing Mabel and me."

"We saw George pushing the envelope into your jacket pocket. Just before he was knifed."

Dottie made up her mind. "All right, Billy. I believe you, but we haven't finished with you yet. You might not have intended to do Mabel and me any harm, but you scared us following us around like that and caused Mabel to run her car off the road into a tree. We might have been killed." She found a pen and piece of paper in her purse and handed it to Billy. "Write down your phone number."

Billy looked at Dottie. "What for?"

"You'll see. And don't try to pull any fast ones. We have... connections." She cleared her throat. "With the police. They'd be happy to know what you and Den have been up to."

He scribbled down a number and gave it to Dottie. She put it in her handbag. "By the way, the Harley is fabulous."

Billy's face broke into a rare smile, exposing the missing tooth. "I've had it for two years now."

"I'm referring to the one you and Enrique found for me."

Billy's eyes widened. "I don't know no... Enric."

"You made a deal with him to find me a Harley."

He laughed nervously. "What you talkin' about? I don't do no deals in bikes."

Dottie persisted. "It was a few weeks ago at Yolanda's stables."

Grabbing his jacket, Billy stood up to leave. "You musta got me confused with someone else."

As she watched him sidle out of the pub, Dottie felt sick. Billy was a liar, but he'd seemed genuinely puzzled about a bike deal and claimed he didn't know anyone called Enrique.

When he left, Mabel burst out laughing. "Connections with the police! That was a good one, Dottie!"

"What?" Dottie shook herself. "Well, I don't trust Billy, even though he's no more than a petty thief. It doesn't do any harm to use a bit of scare tactics now and again. And who knows when we might want to make use of his services?"

CHAPTER 18

They left the city right after breakfast. Alarm bells went off when Muggins didn't run to greet Dottie at the front door, until she remembered that, since the kidnapping, he often curled up on her bed, not bothering to show up until he grew hungry. Still, it wouldn't hurt to check.

As she headed to the bedroom, the back doorbell rang. It was her neighbour Margaret. "Oh, Dottie!" she cried, dabbing her eyes with a tissue.

"What's the matter?" Dottie exclaimed. That started another spate of tears. "Come on in, I'll make us some coffee."

"I can't! I—I don't know what to say!"

Dottie, tired from the weekend's excitement, didn't have the patience to deal with the dithering Margaret. "For Pete's sake, come into the house!" Her stomach clenched when she saw the cat collar in Margaret's hand. "Oh, my God—it's Muggins, isn't it?" Her voice cracked. "What happened? Is he—did he run into the road?"

"It's nothing like that. When I let myself into the house last night around six to give him his dinner, he must have been waiting. He shot past me into the garden. I didn't have a chance to catch him." She blew her nose loudly. "I searched for an hour. I found his collar on the back porch."

Dottie closed her eyes and took a deep breath. "OK, we'll both look for him." What with the kidnapping, then being confined inside the house because of the cat killer, it didn't surprise Dottie that Muggins had waited for a chance to escape.

They knocked on neighbours' doors and, using a flashlight, searched under hedges and down dark alleys. Margaret phoned the Humane Society to see if a cat fitting Muggins' description had been found. No, the receptionist told her, but she assured Margaret that most cats find their way home within a day or two. Dottie posted a notice on a tree at the end of her driveway, offering a reward for the safe return of a "lovable ginger cat named Muggins." She added in the word *lovable* hoping it would stir emotions, but she really couldn't describe Muggins as lovable. He wasn't one for cuddling, preferring to spend his time in the garden, stalking birds, although he did allow Margaret to pick him up and sometimes sat on her lap. He's probably hiding in some quiet spot away from people, Dottie told herself, blinking back tears. She refused to dwell on her worst fear.

When Margaret left, Dottie lit a cigarillo. She paced the living room, her eyes scanning the garden each time she passed the window. The phone rang. She could let the answering machine pick up the message. Still, it might be Enrique, and after the conversation with Billy last evening, she wanted some answers.

Dottie checked Call Display. It was Mabel. Squishing out the cigarillo in an ashtray, she picked up the receiver. Mabel sounded very serious. "Dottie, can you come over to my house right away? There's something important I want to show you."

***

When Dottie walked through the door, Mabel handed her a newspaper cutting. Under the headline "Man Robbed at Maple Leaf Mall" was a small photograph of a Mr. Charles Gonzalez, the owner of Chicken Licken. *That's probably Charlie*, Dottie thought. The article described a robbery that had taken place in the Maple Leaf Mall about 7: 30 p.m. last Wednesday. "Mr. Gonzalez was climbing into his car when he was robbed. The assailant wore a stocking over his face," it stated. A caption under the article's picture described a visibly shaken Mr. Gonzalez who refused to speak to the press.

"When you told me about taking the jewelry to Chicken Licken, it rang a bell," Mabel said. "I knew that I'd read something in our local paper about a robbery. I got home and rooted through last week's newspapers."

Dottie's mind began to race. "When I took the emeralds to Chicken Licken, Enrique was hiding behind a dumpster, looking out for me." She paused. "So he said." Could Enrique have attacked Charlie? Surely, he wasn't capable of stooping so low; but then, how much did she know about him?

Despite her reluctance to admit that Enrique might be guilty of the theft, it began to make sense. If Enrique robbed Charlie and made off with what he believed were the real emeralds, no wonder she hadn't heard from him! But why had he bothered to get the jewelry copied in the first place? He'd had the real emeralds for more than a week and could have absconded with them without going through the rigmarole of making copies. He'd also risked being caught by the police when he'd robbed Charlie.

She phoned Enrique at his business number. When the answering machine kicked in, she left a simple message. "It's Dottie. Please call."

***

Dottie threw herself into work and attacked the backlog that had built up while she'd been away in Unionville looking after her grandchildren. It helped to keep her mind off Enrique. As expected, Enrique hadn't returned her call, and by the end of the week, she'd given up on him.

Dottie concentrated on finding Muggins. He'd been missing for more than a week now, and she prayed that he would turn up. She phoned the Humane Society every day. Each morning before breakfast, she searched in the garden calling his name, and when she got home from work, she looked out the window in the faint hope he would be sitting by the back door. Margaret also searched for him and phoned neighbours in the off chance he'd been spotted.

Dottie checked the local paper every day to see if any more cats had been poisoned. Nothing was mentioned. Perhaps the cat killer had moved on to another community. If that were the case, maybe Muggins had been spared.

By the time Friday rolled around, it occurred to her that she hadn't heard from Mabel. Dottie phoned several times, but the answering machine picked up. Had her friend taken ill? Mabel had a very active social life, but she lived alone. Knowing Mabel's weakness for romance novels, Dottie visited Chapters at lunchtime, picked up a Harlequin paperback, and drove over to the house.

When Mabel opened the door, Dottie sensed something was wrong. At first, she couldn't pinpoint the problem. Mabel's hair looked freshly washed and set, and she wore a bright yellow dress and red sandals. Nothing unusual about that. And there was nothing unusual about her bright coral pink lipstick and turquoise eye shadow. The blank expression on Mabel's face and puffiness around her eyes alarmed Dottie.

"What's happened, Mabel?"

"It's a long story," she sniffed, dabbing her nose with a tissue. "Come in."

As Dottie entered the living room, she noticed a glass of sherry and a half empty bottle of Bristol Cream on the coffee table.

"I'll put some coffee on," Dottie said. "Or would you prefer tea?"

"Coffee's fine," came the meek reply.

Soon, the familiar smell of fresh coffee permeated the air. When it was perked, Dottie poured two generous mugs and added cream and sugar to Mabel's. She returned to the living room.

"Try to drink this," she urged.

Mabel took the mug and nursed it with both hands. "How could I have been so naive! I knew he was troubled about something, but I never expected this."

Dottie sat beside her friend and waited. She must be referring to her brother Giles. Giles had been in and out of jail since he was a teenager, and he only got in touch with Mabel when he wanted money. After the last attempt to extract funds from his sister, Mabel made it clear that she didn't want any more to do with him. He must have contacted her again. "Giles isn't worth troubling yourself over, Mabel. He's given you nothing but aggravation since he was a young boy."

"We haven't spoken for ages. I'm not talking about Giles. It's Vincenzo." Tears sprang into her eyes again.

"Vincenzo?"

"I haven't heard from him in weeks, so I called his office. I was transferred to someone called Des, who told me that Vincenzo is no longer involved in the car dealership business. When I asked him if he had any idea of his whereabouts, Des said he didn't know."

Dottie put her arm around her friend's shoulder. "I'm sorry, Mabel."

Mabel took a few sips of coffee. "The thing is that I liked Vincenzo. He was very considerate and always treated me with respect. Since Alf died, I haven't really bothered much. Just the odd dinner date here and there. Then, Vincenzo came along. I thought it might have developed into something more than friendship." She paused. "We had some good times. I'm going to miss him."

"I know what you mean," agreed Dottie. "I feel much the same way about Enrique. I left a message for Enrique last week and haven't heard back."

The two women sat in silence for a while, each lost in their own thoughts. "Well," Dottie said at last. "I must get back to work." She picked up her car keys. "I'll tell you what. A new restaurant just opened in the city, part of an Australian chain. It has a giant TV screen, old-fashioned booths, and plays live music on the weekends."

"It sounds like the kind of place we could both do with at the moment," Mabel said.

"I'll book for Saturday evening. We'll drink ice cold beer and eat pizza."

Mabel's face brightened. "And watch the hockey game."

"You're on! Oh, and no arguments, I'm driving."

Mabel smiled. "That sounds even better."

CHAPTER 19

As it turned out, *Roos* didn't take bookings over the phone. "Get here early, and you'll get a table." The man sounded very young and spoke with an Australian accent. "Or leave it until later, say around 8:30. That's when the live music starts."

Dottie began to have second thoughts. Perhaps they should try to find somewhere quieter.

"Tell you what. Get here around 8:15, and I'll make sure you get a good table. My name's Mike; just ask for me when you arrive."

"Sounds good. I'm Dottie Flowers. And it's for two."

"Right you are."

Dottie replaced the phone. *What do you wear at a place like that?* she wondered. I'd better go and check out my wardrobe. Something casual...

***

After they'd been seated, the two women ordered beers and pizza. The bright lighting in the restaurant dimmed when the band was introduced. Multicoloured strobe lights flashed as Bobby and the Kings opened with a loud rendition of a Beatles number.

"It's warm in here!" shouted Mabel.

"What did you say?"

Mabel waved her hand dismissively. "Tell you later!"

144

Dottie and Mabel sat opposite each other in the small booth, sipping cold beer. They'd ordered a vegetarian pizza fifteen minutes ago, but there was no sign of their waiter. "He's probably flirting with those cheerleaders who came in right after us," Mabel remarked. They looked around the large dining room. It wasn't easy to see with the flashing lights. "I was right!" Mabel pointed to a young man surrounded by a group of cheerleaders dressed in emerald green outfits.

Five minutes later, the pizza arrived. "Mmm." Mabel helped herself to a slice. "I can't remember the last time I ate pizza."

Dottie sighed with pleasure as she breathed in the delicious aroma of peppers mingled with hot cheese. "This smells divine."

As she was about to bite into it, a woman's raised voice caught her attention. It came from the booth behind her. "I've had enough of this crap, Tom! You've gone too far this time!"

"Someone's not happy," Mabel whispered.

Dottie placed the pizza slice on her plate. Where had she heard that voice before? It was loud and grating, very distinctive. Graciana—that was it. Graciana, Enrique's niece!

"We had a deal, Tom," the voice ground on. "Once you got your hands on the jewelry, we were going to live in Spain. The two of us, you said. Huh!"

"Keep your voice down!"

"I don't care who hears! And don't try to tell me you were planning to take me with you! I found your plane ticket; remember!" The man gave a muffled response.

"I need a drink," Graciana demanded.

145

"I'll get the waiter's attention. Do you want whisky or one of those martini specials that you like, my dear. Or what about a Spanish coffee? They make good…"

Graciana cut in. "Don't try and get around me, Tom. Just order a double whisky, and be quick about it."

Dottie began to feel queasy. The man's voice was a bit rough, but there was no mistaking it. "It's Enrique!" whispered Dottie.

"What do you mean?" Mabel spluttered. "It can't be Enrique. It's Vincenzo! I would recognize his voice anywhere!"

The two women stared at each other. Surely, it wasn't possible! Numbly, Dottie turned around. Her face pink with anger, Graciana was tapping long fingernails on the table. Her partner sat with his back to them but turned when the waiter arrived. Dottie's heart lurched. When the lights flashed, she saw the telltale scar on his chin.

She turned to Mabel who was halfway out of her seat, trying to get a better view. "Mabel, we have to leave."

"If you think for one minute," Mabel spluttered, " that— that lowlife is going to get away with this…"

"Listen to me." Dottie lowered her voice. "We will make Tom whatever his name is pay, but now's not the time. We need to come up with something that will teach him a lesson he won't forget. He doesn't know we've seen him, so we have the upper hand."

Mabel glared at Dottie. "I don't want to wait. That—that snake deserves to be humiliated!"

"Mabel, trust me. He will be sorry he ever met us, but we need to be patient."

For a few moments, Mabel didn't move. Then, she sighed and sat down again. "I suppose you're right."

"OK," Dottie said, "let's go."

146

As they squeezed out of the booth, Tom spoke. "Going somewhere?" Dottie froze.

"Well, if it isn't Tom Snead," a man's raucous voice replied. "Long time no see!".

"Well, Jimmy Onassis, my old friend! What are you doing in this neck of the woods?"

Dottie grabbed Mabel's arm. "That was a close call. Let's get out of here before he sees us."

"What about the bill?"

"I'll find the waiter. You go ahead. I'll tell him we have to leave right away, as I've got a migraine." *That wouldn't be too far from the truth*, Dottie thought. Her head was spinning and she felt a bit sick. With all the excitement, Graciana wasn't the only one in need of a drink.

***

Back in Dottie's house, she poured them each a generous measure of brandy. Mabel's face had grown very pale, but a couple of sips brought her colour back. "That feels better. I feel like a real idiot letting myself be conned like that. He seemed so genuine."

Dottie thought back to the day that Enrique... Tom (she must stop thinking of him as Enrique) had waltzed into her office—tall, dark, and very good-looking. He'd wanted her to find an apartment in downtown Toronto for his niece. Some niece! She couldn't believe she fell for that one! Dottie, with her excellent reputation as a real estate salesperson, had been highly recommended, he'd told her. As Dottie took her work very seriously, it had been flattering to have her expertise validated.

"Don't be too hard on yourself," Dottie urged. "I was taken in as well. I didn't stop to think who'd recommended me and why he would have chosen a small privately owned company rather than one of the big well-established firms in the city. Tom flattered me, and I fell for it."

"I keep thinking how Vincenzo – I mean Tom – miraculously appeared when I arrived at the club that day," Mabel said. "When he told me that he knew all about cars and owned a car dealership, it seemed like providence, because I knew I had to get a new vehicle. If only I had stopped to think!" She sipped the brandy.

"Look at us beating ourselves up because we fell for Tom's charm," she said. "Just like that woman in Victoria you told me about."

"Yolanda always says if it sounds too good to be true, it probably is."

Yolanda's right, thought Dottie. Providence hadn't brought Tom to the car park that day, Dottie realized. She remembered telling him about Mabel's obsession with her car. He must have found out where Mabel lived and followed her to the club. Posing as the owner of a car dealership was an ideal way to gain her confidence. Knowing that Dottie would be away for a few weeks babysitting her grandchildren, he didn't have to worry about bumping into her when he took Mabel out.

"He had me believing that Graciana was his niece," Dottie said. "Then, he conned me into getting the jewelry copied. I still can't figure out why."

"I know what you mean. He had the chance to steal the antique jewelry Aunt Augustine left me, but he brought it back with an appraisal, as he promised he would." Mabel took a gulp of brandy. "Oh, dear! What if the jewelry is fake? Maybe he had copies made, kept the real jewelry, and handed the fake stuff to me." She stared into space for a few moments.

"What about the car?"

Mabel turned back to Dottie, her eyes full of alarm. "Do you think the car was stolen?"

Dottie sat on the sofa beside Mabel. "Maybe. Let's face it. We've both been taken for a ride. No pun intended." They sipped their brandy in silence.

The rustle of the evening newspaper being pushed through the letterbox broke their reverie. Dottie retrieved it and glanced at the headlines, *"Armed Robbery in Rosedale."* She flicked her eyes over the article. Some jewelry with a couple of valuable paintings had been stolen from a house in Rosedale.

"The police believe this is the work of the same thieves who stole the emerald-and-diamond necklace and earring set which had once belonged to the Tsar of Russia, purported to be worth two million dollars. The tsar's jewelry, stolen from a country estate near Lake Simcoe, has since been found and is now in the hands of the police."

Dottie handed the paper to Mabel. "Look at this!"

Mabel read the article. "Now, we know why we were pursued so rigorously by Den and Billy."

"Never mind Den and Billy. They're small-time crooks. I bet they don't have any idea how much the jewelry is worth. Tom certainly knows. So does the Skinner gang." Dottie looked at Mabel. "If we play our cards right, we can teach Tom Snead a lesson."

"How?"

"Tom thinks he has the real jewelry." Dottie explained how she'd given the wrong envelope to Charlie. "So, after robbing Charlie, Tom ended up with the fake jewelry."

"And the police ended up with the real stuff."

"Yes."

Mabel yawned. "Have you got any ideas how we can teach Tom a lesson?"

"I'm not sure yet, but we know something he doesn't. We'll make him suffer. We need to have clear heads before we decide what to do."

"You're right." Mabel stifled another yawn. "I feel as if I've been through the wringer." She glanced at her watch. "I must phone for a taxi."

"I've got a spare bed made up, and I'll find you a nightdress and toothbrush. You're staying here. "

Mabel smiled sleepily. "Thanks, Dottie."

"Don't worry, Mabel. We'll beat those crooks at their own game!"

***

The next morning, after doing her morning search for Muggins, Dottie bustled around the kitchen, making coffee. She took out her white china decorated with red poppies and set the table, making sure that the mugs and juice glasses were evenly spaced and the white linen napkins neatly folded. As she prepared French toast, Dottie heard Mabel shuffle into the kitchen. Without turning around, she called out, "Sleep well?"

"Very. Despite everything, I'm hungry. Are you making what I think you're making?"

"Yes."

"You make the best French toast. Let me pour the coffee."

Frying pan in hand, Dottie walked over to the table and placed a serving of toast on each plate. "Let's eat while it's hot."

After pouring the coffee, Mabel slathered maple syrup over the toast and cut it into bite-sized pieces. She forked a piece into her mouth. "Mmm! It's as good as I remember!"

Dottie liked to read her newspaper over breakfast. She sipped her coffee and tried to concentrate, but after reading the same headline three times, she put the paper down. "I've been awake half the night thinking about what we should do," she said. "The Skinner gang is dangerous, Mabel. I think we should go to the police and tell them everything we know."

"You've changed your tune. Last night, you were all set to fight back. 'We'll beat those crooks at their own game,' I think you said. Besides, you've always avoided anything to do with the police."

"Yes, well, I've had second thoughts. Not that I look forward to going to the police again. Once was enough."

"I've got an idea." As Mabel leaned across the table, the sleeve of her floral dressing gown landed in the maple syrup on her plate. "Oh, dear, what a mess." She rubbed the sleeve with the table napkin. "That's better. Now, where was I?"

"You said you've got an idea. I'm not sure I want to hear about it because we're in enough trouble as it is."

"Just listen to what I have to say. If you don't agree, then we'll do as you suggest and call the police."

Dottie picked at her French toast. "Go on."

"I think we should track down Tom and confront him."

"How are we supposed to do that?"

"We could get Billy to track him down."

"Why Billy?"

"He and Tom have one thing in common, remember. The stolen jewelry."

Dottie sat up straight. "Hmm... I hadn't thought of that." She looked at Mabel's encouraging smile. "Now, where did I put his phone number?"

CHAPTER 20

Dottie sipped her coffee absentmindedly. Cup in hand, she wandered over to the sunroom, where orchids and other tropical plants flourished under her tender care. Passing a critical eye over the plants to see if any of them needed water, she caught sight of the wrought-iron love seat with its chintz cushions. Her eyes filled with tears. Muggins had always sat on the seat when he'd watched out for mice and birds through the window. It had been almost two weeks since his disappearance, and as each day went by, her hopes of ever seeing him again diminished. He might well be a victim of the serial cat killer, but if that were the case, why hadn't his body been found?

She remembered the morning four years ago when he'd arrived on her doorstep, all skin and bones. He'd meowed and scratched the door, until she took pity on him and gave him a bowl of milk. Although he didn't have an identification tag, she'd contacted the local SPCA in case someone reported a missing orange-striped cat. No one did, so he stayed.

Marching back to the kitchen, she poured herself a little more coffee and tried to take her mind off Muggins by thinking about the upcoming confrontation with Tom. Billy had arranged for Tom to meet him at a local pub under the pretext of having a buyer for the stolen jewelry. Unknown to Tom, Dottie and Mabel would be there as well. It was time he got what he deserved.

Dottie rinsed out her cup vigorously and placed it in the dishwasher. She must get ready for work.

Just as she was putting the finishing touches to her makeup, the phone rang. "Dottie, it's Arnold Gateshead."

"Arnold! What a surprise! Are you still at your friend's cottage in Bracebridge?"

"Yes and no."

Something was wrong. "What do you mean yes and no?"

"I'm phoning from the cottage, but I need to get away for a bit." He cleared his throat. "The thing is that Yolanda and I have had a bit of a bust up."

"Oh, dear."

"Jack's cottage—he's the chap I'm staying with—is next door to Yolanda's, and it could be a bit awkward for us both. So, I wanted to ask you a big favour. Could you put me up for a few nights? Or if that's not convenient, perhaps you could recommend a B and B."

Dottie was fond of Arnold. They'd become friends while taking riding lessons together, and Dottie had encouraged Arnold to invite Yolanda out for dinner. He and Yolanda had been dating steadily for the past few weeks, and from what Mabel said, the romance was progressing well. What had gone wrong? Poor Arnold. "Of course, you can stay here."

"Thank you, Dottie. You gave me your address and phone number when we took those riding lessons." He cleared his throat. "I took the liberty of going into MapQuest on Jack's computer, so I know how to get to your house."

"What time do you think you'll get here?"

"I've got an overnight bag packed. I'll be there in a few hours."

Dottie hadn't expected him so soon. "I'll be in work when you arrive, so I'll leave the house key with my next-door neighbour, Gert Bottomley." Gert was not her first choice. She would normally have asked Margaret. However, Margaret burst into tears whenever she and Dottie met, blaming herself for Muggins' disappearance.

Dottie had tried to reason with her. "Muggins is an outdoor cat. He was waiting for a chance to escape, and it was only a matter of time before he succeeded."

Margaret's reply was always the same. "I should have been more careful!"

***

Dottie managed to get away from work half an hour earlier, so she arrived home by 5:00. As she pulled into her driveway, she was surprised to see smoke rising from the chimney; it was only September, a bit early for a fire.

Arnold opened the front door, pipe in hand, slippers on his feet. His eyes twinkled. "Hello, Dottie!" He took her hand. "It's wonderful to see you again."

"It's great to see you as well."

A pair of horn-rimmed glasses sat halfway down his nose. "I saw a packet of cigarillos in the kitchen. I figured if you smoke, you wouldn't object to my pipe."

"No, I quite like pipe smoke. Let's go inside."

As Dottie walked into the bungalow, she breathed in the mouth-watering aroma of onions and garlic. "Smells delicious."

"I took the liberty of making one of my favourite soups," Arnold continued. He looked reassuringly at Dottie. "Don't worry, it's a vegetable soup. I remember your telling me you're a vegetarian."

Dottie removed her jacket and high-heeled shoes in the hallway. Arnold puffed away on his pipe, watching. "Hope you don't mind, but I made a fire. Dismal day, raining, reminded me of London. I always have a fire going at home when it's dull and drizzly outside."

"You managed to find the wood supply then?"

"Yes, thanks to your neighbour, Mrs. Bottomley."

Dottie's ears pricked up. What had Gert been up to now?

"When I picked up the key, she invited me in for tea. Very kind of her. I must have mentioned that I enjoy a nice fire, and she told me you had a good supply of wood in the garage. It was all neatly stacked. Not a piece of wood out of place! I like that."

"Interfering old bag," Dottie muttered under her breath.

"What did you say, Dottie?"

"Oh, nothing."

Dottie wandered into the living room and sank her feet into faux fur mules. She was used to coming home to an empty house, pouring herself a Scotch on the rocks, and relaxing for half an hour before preparing her evening meal. Still, it felt good to walk into the house to the glow of a warm fire and something bubbling on the stove.

"This reminds me of visits to my grandmother's house in Parry Sound," Dottie murmured. "She was from Yorkshire and always had soup on the go—she called it Omnium Gatherum."

"Omnium Gatherum! That's a phrase I haven't heard for years. If I remember correctly, you keep adding things such as left-over vegetables to the soup, and so the flavour changes as the days go by."

"That's right. You never knew what to expect, but it was always good. Anyway, they had a huge stone fireplace, and we—my cousins and I—would sit on the floor around the fire playing card games or Monopoly."

Arnold was in the process of opening a bottle of wine. "No siblings?"

"No."

He popped the cork. "Ah, that's got it!" He poured two glasses and handed one to Dottie. "It's a Pelee Island Merlot. I've developed quite a taste for it since I've been

155

here—what is it—six weeks now?" Arnold made a toast. "Cheers, bottoms up, and all that!" After swallowing a few mouthfuls, Arnold placed his glass on the sideboard. "Must go and check my soup!"

"Shall I set the table?" Dottie called out.

"No need. I've already set places for two in the sunroom."

Shoot! She tried to avoid the sunroom as much as possible these days, as it reminded her too much of Muggins. She was about to protest, but then changed her mind. *He means well,* she thought to herself, *and he's upset about Yolanda.*

***

They'd just finished supper, and already, Arnold was whisking away the dishes. "Arnold, why don't we sit for a while and chat? The dishes can wait."

Arnold's face grew pink. "Can't stand the sight of dirty dishes! It won't take me long to stack the dishwasher. Then, we can relax over a cup of herbal tea."

"I like coffee after my evening meal."

Arnold looked at Dottie over his glasses. "Coffee is very bad for you, particularly at night. Take my word for it; you'll sleep much better after a cup of chamomile tea."

She bit her tongue. She knew he was trying to be helpful, so she let it go. "Chamomile it is."

By the time Arnold had fussed with the tea and stacked the dishwasher the way he liked it, it was 9 o'clock. She was in no mood for a heart-to-heart. Making the excuse she had to be up very early, bade Arnold a hasty goodnight. She closed her bedroom door with a sigh of relief. As fond as she was of Arnold, she wasn't sure how much of him she could take. Still, she reminded herself, it was only for a few days.

***

Famous last words. Only a few days, huh! Arnold had come down with a nasty bout of flu, so she was stuck with him for at least another week. To make matters worse, Arnold and Gert Bottomley had become friends. She is such a sympathetic person, he told Dottie. Listens to everything I have to say. Dottie didn't have the heart to tell him that Gert was just being nosy.

Dottie had come home one night to find that he had completely rearranged her kitchen shelves. "What have you done?"

"It was Gert's idea," Arnold explained. "I told her I wanted to do something to show my appreciation for your kindness."

Dottie had taken a big breath and counted to ten. That woman again! She knows how particular I am about my kitchen. She also knows I won't say anything to Arnold.

Because she felt uneasy in Gert's presence, Dottie wanted to warn Arnold about her, but what could she say? The woman hadn't done anything.

***

One evening, under the influence of the single glass of red wine he permitted himself, Arnold told Dottie about his fight with Yolanda. It had started when he'd decided to spring-clean Yolanda's living room while she worked at the stables. He'd found piles of old magazines, jigsaw puzzles, and games inside a wooden chest. By the time Yolanda got back to the cottage, he'd taken the contents of the chest to the dump. It turned out that the magazines were not just any old magazines; they were Yolanda's prized collection, many of which dated back to the 1900s; and the jigsaw puzzles and games had been in her family for a long time and were like heirlooms.

With a sigh of resignation, Dottie poured steaming chicken soup into the soup bowl, placed the bowl on a tray, and carried it into Arnold's bedroom.

Arnold was propped up in bed by a stack of pillows. The bedclothes were pulled up so high that only his nose and eyes were visible. He looked the picture of misery, and for a moment, she felt sorry for him. Still, she'd had enough of Arnold and his fussy ways and prayed he would be well enough to leave soon—very soon. Dottie placed the tray in front of him, making sure the tray legs were pulled out properly. "Try to drink the chicken soup, Arnold. It's supposed to be good for colds and flu."

He looked at Dottie through red-rimmed eyes. His spoke in a soft nasal voice. "You're very kind."

"It's the least I can do. Can I get you anything else?"

"No, thank you, but could you do me a favour? That picture in front of me..."

Dottie turned around. It was a print painted in vivid reds and greens.

"I can take it down if it bothers you."

"No, it's nothing like that; it's just that—it's crooked."

Dottie looked carefully at the painting and saw that Arnold was right. It was slightly askew. She marched over and straightened it. "How's that?"

"Down to the left a bit. That's better!" He smiled weakly.

Dottie resisted the temptation to slam the bedroom door as she left.

***

A few days later, Arnold had recovered. Dottie cheered up. Soon, she would have the house to herself again. She decided to cook Arnold the one dish she was good at— homemade macaroni and cheese. Humming a favourite tune, she climbed out of her car and grabbed the plastic grocery bags off the backseat.

As she opened the front door, Dottie stopped in her tracks. A sickly sweet smell filled the air, and low voices hummed from the living room. Dottie marched into the room to find Arnold sitting cross-legged on the floor, smoking a toke. Next to him, Fred Fortune, sprawled over the carpet, was rolling another one. Empty wine bottles littered the floor.

A silly grin crossed Arnold's face when he saw Dottie. "Dottie! Come and join the party!" He patted the floor beside him. "He's a good chap is Fred, a good chap! What a stoke— stroke —of luck that he dropped by!"

CHAPTER 21

Dottie had the urge to punch Fred Fortune in the face. "What the hell are you doing!" she demanded. "Someone had better do some explaining. Fast!"

Fred looked at Dottie through glazed eyes. "All my fault. You see..." With a huge effort, he manoeuvred himself into a sitting position. "I decided to drop by. Arnold here..." Fred flung out his arm in the general direction of Arnold, "... invited me in."

"Fred," Dottie tried to keep her voice as even as possible. "Would you please get out of my house, right now, before I call the police?"

"Happy to oblige." Fred struggled to his feet.

A sudden thought struck Dottie. "Where's your car?"

Arnold piped up. "Poor chap had to sell it—short of cash, you know."

"I'll get you a taxi."

"That's kind, Dottie, but no point."

"What do you mean?"

"Fred's been living out of his car," Arnold hiccupped. "Until yesterday, when he ran out of cash."

Dottie let out a long sigh. "OK, this is the deal, Fred. You can stay here for one night. Tomorrow morning, first thing, I want you out of here, and you're not to come back. Ever. Do you understand?"

With a contrite expression on his face, Fred mumbled his thanks.

"And I want both of you to clear up this mess!" Dottie roared. "Now!"

***

Fred escaped to bed right after they'd cleared up the living room. He couldn't even think of eating, he told Dottie. Arnold was about to follow, but Dottie wasn't having any of that. "You've got some explaining to do, Arnold. I've just made some chamomile tea for you and some sandwiches, so sit down."

"Yes, of course." Arnold ran a hand through his thinning hair. "Don't suppose you have any aspirin?"

Dottie produced an aspirin bottle from her medicine cabinet. Arnold removed two pills and swallowed them. "Thanks." He looked at Dottie with bloodshot eyes. "I'm very sorry for the distress I've caused you. I shouldn't have invited Fred into your house, Dottie." He poured himself a cup of tea. "It's just that—well—he convinced me that you and he were old friends, and he was just dropping by to say hello. I must confess I was feeling particularly low when the doorbell rang. I'd just got off the phone from Yolanda."

"And it didn't go well, I presume."

Arnold shook his head. "I phoned her to try to make amends, but she's still very upset with me. Says I'm too uptight. She said I need to chill out a bit."

"I don't think that drinking cheap plonk and smoking marijuana with the likes of Fred Fortune was what she had in mind."

Arnold hung his head. "No."

"Fred can't be trusted." An image of Fred in conversation with Billy flashed into her head. He was probably a thief as well.

"He's fallen on bad times. He owes money to loan sharks…"

"I gave him some money a few weeks ago to help pay his debt. He was coming to see me today to cadge more money, I expect."

Arnold looked crestfallen. They sat in silence for a while, sipping tea. Arnold picked at the sandwiches.

"How's the headache?" Dottie asked.

"It's much better now that the aspirin has kicked in." He rubbed his face. "I'd like to give Fred a second chance, and I've got an idea." Dottie was about to interrupt, but he raised his hand. "We had a long chat this afternoon. He told me he was a lawyer by profession. A good one, by all accounts, until he got into gambling. That was his downfall. When he lost his business, his wife divorced him."

"I didn't know he was divorced." She remembered the pain etched on Fred's face when he'd mentioned his family.

"I got the impression he told me things that he hadn't told anyone else." Arnold settled back in the chair. "Anyway, let me tell you what I have in mind. I do a lot of business with Smith and Day, an international law firm. They are always on the lookout for good people."

She was tempted to tell Arnold she suspected Fred was a thief but decided she'd better speak to Fred first. "You're taking a risk, Arnold. I don't think Fred has had a steady job in years."

"Maybe not, but he's hit rock bottom this time. And he's tired of being in debt and of roaming around. He wants to find a place and put down some roots."

"He told you that?"

"In so many words, yes."

A terrible thought crossed Dottie's mind. "You didn't offer to pay off his debt, did you?"

"Absolutely not. If he has a steady income, he'll be able to pay off the debt quickly. It's up to him."

Dottie thought about Arnold's proposal. It might work, but if it didn't, Fred could still land on her doorstep looking for another handout. As though reading her mind, Arnold leaned towards her, eyes twinkling. "The thing is, Dottie, what I haven't told you is that the company's headquarters is in South America."

The significance of Arnold's words sank in. "Even if Fred doesn't stick with the job, it's a long way from South America to Mississauga."

"Precisely." He stood up. "I'm off to bed. 'Night, Dottie."

"Goodnight, Arnold."

Dottie smiled when she realized that he hadn't attempted to clear away the tea dishes. Was it possible that he was beginning to chill out a bit?

As Dottie cleared away the dishes, she thought about Fred's connection with Billy. Was Fred involved in the stolen wine and the jewelry she'd found at the stables, or were he and Billy casual acquaintances? She yawned. She'd confront him tomorrow. Right now, she needed some sleep.

***

In the morning, Dottie got up early and made a pot of coffee. She sat down with the morning paper. Arnold wandered into the kitchen in his dressing gown, his skin an unhealthy pasty colour.

"You look like you need some coffee."

He massaged his temples. "Don't normally drink the stuff but need something to wake me up."

Dottie handed him a mug of steaming coffee. "I'll see if Fred wants to join us."

She knocked on Fred's bedroom door. No answer. She was about to knock again when she saw a piece of yellow

Post-It paper on the floor. She picked it up. Scrunching her
eyes, she managed to decipher the spidery scrawl.

*Thanks for letting me stay the night, Dottie. It means a
lot. Fred*

The questions Dottie had wanted to ask Fred would
have to wait. She returned to the kitchen.

Arnold sipped his coffee. "Ah, that's good!"

"It seems our friend has already left."

"Fred told me he had to meet someone at Yolanda's
stables first thing this morning."

"Yolanda's stables?"

"He might get a couple of weeks' work there. Casual
labour, but it's better than nothing. The good thing is he
will get room and board if he's taken on."

"Has he worked there before?"

"He's been up there looking for work, but they didn't
need anyone. Someone just left, so he might be in luck."
That'll be Billy, thought Dottie.

Dottie checked her watch. "Speaking of work, I'll be late
if I don't get a move on."

Arnold cleared his throat. "Before you go, I wanted to
tell you I'm leaving tomorrow."

Dottie was taken by surprise. "Where are you going?"

"Back to Bracebridge." He blushed. "The thing is I know
why Yolanda is upset with me. I've been a bachelor too long,
and I'm set in my ways. I'd like to start all over again."

"Have you got anything in mind? To entice her, I mean."

Arnold's face was wreathed in smiles. He pulled a
brochure out of his dressing gown pocket and handed it
to Dottie. She read the headline on the brightly coloured

brochure: Mediterranean Cruises—Take the Woman of Your Dreams on the Cruise of a Lifetime!

"Yolanda has always wanted to go on a Mediterranean cruise, so I'm hoping she'll give me another chance and let me escort her. You see, when she first broached the subject of a cruise, I was reluctant. I've never been on one before. Never been anywhere much, always take my annual holiday in Devon. Except this year. Jack's been trying to get me to come to Canada for years. Not the adventurous type you see. But the travel agent has assured me that cruising is very straightforward; they do everything for you, and if I take some sea sickness pills with me, I should be all right."

"You're prone to seasickness?"

"Don't know. Just thought I should be prepared."

"Well! It all sounds very exciting—and romantic. I'm sure Yolanda will be delighted."

Arnold looked anxiously at Dottie. "Do you really think so?"

"Why don't you give her a call? Tell her you're coming back to Bracebridge, and you have a surprise for her." *Here I go again*, thought Dottie. *Arnold seems to bring out the mother in me.*

"If you think so..."

"It can't do any harm."

Arnold disappeared. Less than a minute later, he was back. "She won't talk to me. Hung up the minute she recognized my voice."

Dottie tried to cheer him up. "Never mind. When you tell her about the cruise, she'll forgive you."

Arnold looked at Dottie in despair. "But what if she doesn't!"

***

165

When Dottie arrived home from work, she expected to find Arnold busily preparing supper. He'd promised to make her a special dinner, as it was his last night in her home, but the house was in darkness, and he was nowhere to be seen. Asparagus, a bag of potatoes, and a whole-wheat baguette lay on the kitchen counter. A piece of notepaper was propped up in front of the baguette.

Gone for a long walk. Needed to clear my head a bit. Dinner's still on me—we'll dine at 8. Arnold.

What an odd note! Arnold didn't go for long walks; he fussed around the house, read the papers, and listened to the radio. And he liked to eat at 6:00, on the dot. *He must be feeling very low,* Dottie concluded. *I'll pour him a Scotch when he gets back. It might help him to relax a bit.*

A loud rap on the sunroom door made Dottie jump. Who was that? Hardly anyone came to the back door. She saw the outline of man at the window. A jolt of fear skittered down her spine, even though the door was locked with double bolts. She wished Arnold hadn't gone for that walk.

Another rap. This time, a man's voice called out, "Dottie! It's Arnold. Let me in!"

She breathed a sigh of relief. "Come round to the front door," she called out. "This one's a bit tricky to open."

"I'd rather not. You'll see why when you open the door."

What was he up to? "All right. You'll have to be patient, as the bolt's rusty." It was more difficult than she'd imagined, and she cursed when one of her long fingernails broke. "This had better be worth it," Dottie muttered.

Finally, the bolt gave way, and she opened the door. Her eyes fell on the bundle of orange fur cradled in Arnold's arms. "I believe this is Muggins," he grinned.

At the sound of his name, Muggins let out a loud meow, leapt out of Arnold's arms, and bolted into the house.

***

Muggins brushed himself against Dottie's legs, purring loudly. After a large dish of cat food, he curled up in front of the fire and fell asleep. Dottie looked at him affectionately. His fur was a mess, and he was a bit thin, but it wouldn't be long before he was back to his old self again.

Over a glass of wine, Arnold told Dottie what had happened. He'd been for a walk and was about turn into Dottie's driveway when Gert Bottomley waylaid him. Her neighbour, Nellie Yokes, had just returned from a two-week visit with her sister in Kitchener and was afraid to open the garage door because there were scratching sounds coming from inside.

"So, I told Gert to grab a flashlight, and we walked over to Nellie's house," Arnold explained. "When I opened the garage door, I found Muggins."

"How did you manage to catch him? Didn't he try to run away?"

"He was stuck on a shelf at the top of the garage. He wouldn't stop meowing until I climbed up and rescued him."

"How could he survive without water or food?"

"Nellie likes to leave food for the neighbourhood cats, so there was a large bag of dry cat food in the garage. It had a small hole in the bottom—probably mice—and some pellets fell out. As for water, the garage roof leaks. Nellie had placed a small plastic container to catch any water that came through the garage roof. With all the rain we've been having lately, the container was almost full."

"I can't begin to thank you..."

"No, Dottie, it is I who should be thanking you. And now, you relax for half an hour while I prepare dinner."

***

After a delightful dinner of poached salmon, new potatoes, and asparagus, accompanied by a bottle of wine, it was getting late. Dottie wouldn't let Arnold do any clearing up. She insisted that, since he had a long drive in the morning, he must get a good night's rest. He finally gave in and went to bed.

When she heard Arnold's bedroom door close, Dottie picked up the phone. She punched in Yolanda's number. "This is Dottie Flowers, Yolanda. I need to tell you something."

"Yes? What is it? Is it Arnold—is he all right?"

"Yes, Arnold's fine. Listen to me." As Dottie described Arnold's heroic feat, she had no qualms about embellishing the facts. By the time she'd finished, it sounded as if Arnold had risked life and limb to rescue Muggins.

Yolanda began to make strange noises in her throat. It took Dottie a minute to realize that she was trying not to cry. In a quivery voice, Yolanda told Dottie how much she missed Arnold, and how awful she'd been to him. He would never forgive her. Would Dottie try to persuade him that she really didn't mean what she said, that he could be as fussy as he liked, she didn't care. She just wanted him back.

CHAPTER 22

Dottie and Mabel met Billy at The Bluebell the following evening, as arranged. By the time they arrived, Billy was already halfway through a bottle of beer. He took a swig and wiped his hand across his mouth. "The meeting's set for next Thursday evening at 7 o'clock in Da Vinci's."

"That's good," Dottie said, "but how can you be sure he'll show up?"

"I told 'im I might have an interested buyer for the jewelry."

"That doesn't surprise me one bit!" Mabel exclaimed. She would have said more, but at that moment, she felt a sharp dig in her ribs. She looked up to find Dottie glaring at her. Mabel took a deep breath. "I mean, from what you've told us, Tom sounds like an unsavoury character."

"I could tell you stories..."

"We're not interested," Dottie interrupted. "Just tell us about this place. Does it have booths?"

"Booths and low lighting."

"Perfect. So, you'll get there in plenty of time to secure a booth with a good view of the door. We'll arrive about 6:30."

"You sure you know what you're doin'?"

"Oh, yes, we know what we're doing!" Mabel's eyes gleamed.

Billy downed his last mouthful of beer. "OK, if you say so." He grabbed his jacket and sidled out the back door.

"What are we going to say to Tom?" Dottie wondered. "Give us back the jewelry or else?"

"I don't think we'll have any problem thinking of what to say. It's time he got his comeuppance."

"You know," Dottie grinned, "I'm actually looking forward to Thursday!"

***

Over the next few days, Dottie and Mabel discussed their strategy, and by the time Thursday rolled around, they were well prepared for the confrontation. Even so, their initial bravado had evaporated a bit. They were dealing with criminals and con artists, and lurking in the background was the dreaded Skinner gang.

As she got dressed, Dottie was all fingers and thumbs. After stabbing herself twice trying to put on a pair of diamond earrings, she opted to wear her amber clip-ons instead. She applied makeup with great care, concealed the crow's feet under her eyes with special camouflage cream, and brushed her hair until it shone. She toyed with the idea of putting it into a bun but decided that was too harsh. Allowing her hair to hang loosely on her shoulders was sexier. She took a good look at herself in the mirror. A tight-fitting black skirt and royal blue silk sweater flattered her slim figure, and black stockings and high heels enhanced her long legs. A dash of deep cinnamon lipstick and she was ready. Her confidence restored, she fed Muggins, grabbed her black purse, and marched out of the house.

She picked Mabel up in the BMW. "You look very snazzy, Mabel," Dottie remarked as her friend stepped into the car wearing a green silk dress and gold high-heeled sandals. Her hair was perfectly styled and her makeup carefully applied.

Mabel's eyes glanced over Dottie's outfit. "You're looking pretty snazzy yourself."

One thing was certain. She and Mabel looked like women of the world who would never be taken in by good looks and smooth talk. And by the time they'd dealt with Tom, he would be sorry he ever set eyes on them.

Dottie smiled. "Tom is in for a big shock!" *Let's hope we aren't in for a big shock*, Dottie thought. She pushed all negative thoughts to the back of her mind as she backed out of Mabel's driveway; but when she drove into the Da Vinci parking lot, her heart began to race. She glanced over at Mabel and noticed she looked a bit pale.

"Are you all right, Mabel?"

"Yes, it's a bit nerve-racking, that's all."

"Let's look at it as an adventure. We've never been ones to shy away from a challenge, have we?"

"You're right!" Mabel managed a weak smile.

Dottie glanced at her watch. It was almost 6:30. "OK, let's go!"

***

Dottie's eyes took a few seconds to become accustomed to the dimly lit interior of Da Vinci. The pungent smell of cigar smoke surprised her, since most eating establishments frowned upon cigar smoking. In fact, all smoking had just recently been banned from restaurants and bars in the area. Obviously, Da Vinci's had chosen to ignore the new law. Raucous laughter occasionally broke the hum of voices as harassed waiters rushed back and forth.

The walls were painted the colour of saffron and decorated with posters of Venice, Rome, and the Italian Riviera. Large wooden booths had been built all along them. Dottie felt relieved to see Billy sitting in a booth within sight of the front door. He was hunched over a menu, his eyes darting nervously over the pages. The two women made their way over to the booth and sat down opposite him.

"What do you want to drink?" Dottie asked.

Billy ran his hands through his straggly hair. "A beer."

"What time is Tom due to arrive?"

"Seven."

The server came to their booth. "One beer, please." Dottie said. "And two diet ginger ales with lots of ice." They needed their wits about them when they confronted Tom.

She glanced at her watch. "It's 6:49."

Billy and Mabel looked anxiously at their watches. "I have 6:50," Mabel said.

"Mine says 6:52."

It was funny, but no one was in the mood to laugh.

Billy bit nervously on his thumbnail. "What if Tom sees you sitting 'ere with me when 'e walks in?"

"Good point," Dottie remarked, and she and Mabel turned slightly towards the wall so that Tom would only see the backs of their heads. "You let us know when he comes through the door."

The drinks were served, and the three of them lapsed into silence. Dottie drummed her fingers on the tabletop. This was worse than sitting in the dentist's, waiting for a root canal. By the time 7 o'clock rolled around, Dottie's stomach was in knots. She heard Billy's intake of breath and forced herself not to turn around. "Is it Tom?" her voice rasped.

"No."

She glanced quickly towards the door. A man, woman, and two children stood at the entrance and looked around. The man pointed to the empty booth behind Dottie, Mabel, and Billy.

When the four arrived at the booth, the boy whined, "I don't want to sit here!"

A girl's voice, just as whiny, joined in. "I wanna sit by the window!"

"Sit down and behave yourself, Jimmy! And June, stop grizzling!" the woman's sharp voice ordered.

The noisy chatter as the parents tried to calm down their offspring was a welcome relief to Dottie. She wasn't sure how much longer her nerves would hold out.

"He just walked in," Billy whispered.

Dottie's heart pounded, and she felt light-headed. Although she knew it was too risky to turn around, her curiosity got the better of her, and she moved her head very slightly, enough for a sideways view. Even dressed casually in a pair of jeans and leather jacket, Dottie recognized Tom at once. With his striking good looks, he looked like he belonged on a film set. What was the expression Serena had used to describe him? Eye candy. Dottie found herself agreeing with Serena as she watched him saunter across the room towards them.

Mabel kept her head down, while Dottie turned to the side and pretended to search for something in her purse.

When Tom drew close to the booth, he stopped. "I see you have company."

Dottie and Mabel turned to him in unison. "Enrique!" cried Dottie. "Fancy seeing you here!"

"Vincenzo!" cried Mabel. "What a surprise!"

Tom's jaw dropped.

"Do sit down, Enrique!" Dottie ordered. "You look as if you've seen a ghost."

Tom sank down next to Billy, his eyes glued on the two women.

"I think you could do with a drink, Vincenzo," Mabel piped up. "Chianti, if I remember correctly." She nodded to the server who came to their table. "A glass of Chianti for this... gentleman, please!"

"I think a full-bodied Spanish wine might be a better choice." Dottie broke in. She was beginning to enjoy herself.

"Well, what's it to be?" snapped the server.

"A brandy," croaked Tom. "Make it a double."

"I think," Dottie said, her eyes pinned on Tom, "that you have a lot of explaining to do." Tom shifted in his seat, eyes averted. As she waited for his response, Dottie felt someone's breath on her neck. She turned around. A brawny man in a striped business suit stood by the booth. His massive arms and chest were too big for the suit jacket, which looked as if it were about to split open at the seams. Long grey hair was tied back at the nape of his thick neck.

"Move over, lady!" he hissed.

Dottie was about to protest when Billy spoke. "Do as he says, Dottie." The look of fear on Billy's face was enough. She shuffled along the bench to make room, and the man squeezed in beside her.

"Well, well!" he smirked, his eyes darting around the booth. Like brown bullets, his eyes bored into Dottie. "Mrs. Dottie Flowers, isn't it? You and your friend here," he nodded his head in Mabel's direction, "are getting yourselves quite a reputation."

Dottie's palms began to sweat.

He turned his attention to Tom. "And if it isn't Tom Snead! How's that wife of yours?"

Tom didn't respond.

"Listen up," the man snarled. "We got some talking to do. I got plenty of time, so I'm staying until I get the answers I'm after."

Dottie bristled. "Who do you think you are ordering us around! This is a free country!"

The man's voice dropped, so it was barely audible. "It don't matter who I am, lady. I'm here to get the emeralds, and I'm not leaving until I do."

"Well, I don't intend to sit here and be ordered around!" Dottie stood up.

"Lady, you ain't going nowhere." His eyes narrowed into slits. "If anyone thinks of leaving, think again. I have a gun, and one wrong move from any of you, and you're toast!"

"Rocco, I gotta go for a pee..." Billy's voice came out as a squeak.

So, this was Rocco, leader of the Skinner gang! Dottie sat, grabbed her ginger ale, and gulped it down.

Rocco waved his hand impatiently at Billy. "Be quick." When Billy left, he thumped the table with a meaty fist. "Now, listen up! Whoever has the emeralds must cough up now or else!" He ran his forefinger across his throat. "You get my message?"

All four heads nodded in unison. Rocco settled back in his seat. He removed a cigar from his breast pocket and proceeded to light it just as the server arrived with the drinks.

She looked at Rocco. "The usual?" she drawled, her mouth curved in a half-smile.

"Yeah, Betty. Better make it a triple," he grinned, exposing a mouthful of gold teeth. "We could be here a while."

An uneasy silence settled on the small group when the server walked away. As Dottie sipped the ginger ale, she thought about how frightened poor Muggins must have been when he was captured, shoved into that cramped box, and kept there for days by the Skinner gang. Their leader,

Rocco, had a lot to answer for. "Do you always go around threatening people to get what you want?"

His eyes fixed on Dottie. "Lady, most people don't ask questions. They just do as they're told."

"What about George Fernandes—didn't he do as he was told?" She took a deep breath. "Was that why you killed him?"

"Who told you that?"

"It's obvious, isn't it. You and your... friends were at the casino. You followed George, and when I won the jackpot and the lights started to flash, it was the diversion you needed."

"Well, well. Quite the detective, aren't we?" He took a long drag on his cigar. "I got news for you, lady. Even if we planned to get rid of him, as you claim—I'm not saying we did, mind—someone else saved us the trouble."

"What do you mean?"

"I mean that by the time my colleagues got to your machine—to see what your winnings was, you understand—George was dead meat."

"Dead meat?"

"Lyin' on the floor with a knife in his back."

CHAPTER 23

G reta watched Tom put on his leather jacket and grab the car keys from the kitchen counter. When his Mustang pulled out of the driveway, she reached for her coral pink leather jacket, checked to make sure her car keys were in the pocket, and dashed out to her late model Porsche. It didn't take long to catch up. She felt a rush of adrenaline as she trailed Tom's Mustang. She'd always enjoyed living dangerously, and there'd been plenty of that when she ran with the Skinner gang—drugs, parties, hard rock, and frequent run-ins with the police. That was years ago, but some things stay with you.

Her hands tightened on the leather-covered steering wheel. He'd done this once too often. Going to meet a business associate, he said. She didn't trust Tom as far as she could throw him. It was lucky that she'd found the one-way ticket to Costa Del Sol. Tom always was careless about leaving things around. When she'd confronted him, he'd admitted he'd planned to take the jewelry and live the good life on the Spanish Riviera. She'd lost her temper and thrown that vase at him. He had a nasty cut under his eye. Served him right.

Tonight he was in for a big surprise. Greta eased up on the accelerator as Tom signalled a right turn and pulled into the parking lot of Da Vinci's. She parked her car well away from Tom's Mustang, as close to the exit as possible. She might need a quick getaway. Using the car mirror, she checked her makeup and put on fresh lipstick. Her hair had been washed and set and nails manicured to perfection— long, sleek, bright pink, just the way she liked them. The morning at the beauty salon had been well spent. With a black spandex top, short figure-hugging skirt, coral pink slingbacks, and matching jacket, Greta felt like a million dollars. She intended to keep on living the high life, and no one was going to stop her. Tom was about to discover that nobody messed around with her and got away with it.

She walked up the steps and was about to open the restaurant door when the maitre d' opened it for her. His smile quickly faded. "Mrs. Snead! Er, good evening!"

"Good evening, Rolando," Greta smiled. "I'm looking for my husband."

Rolando swallowed hard. "I'm not sure..."

At that moment, Greta caught sight of Tom sitting at one of the booths. A woman sat opposite him, but all Greta could see was the woman's blond hair. "Don't worry. I've found him."

Many customers turned to watch her as she sashayed across the room, her three-inch slingbacks clicking on the tiles. She was still a looker and knew it. Tom had better have a good excuse ready. As she approached the booth, it occurred to her that it might be smart to see what was going on before she confronted him. The more ammunition, the better.

She found a table close enough, but not too close, to where Tom was sitting.

"May I get you anything to drink?" the young waiter smiled.

She needed a clear head. "A Perrier on ice with a slice of lime, please."

While she waited for her drink, she glanced over at the booth. Next to Tom sat that creep Billy, a small-time crook who, with his buddy Den, had been a thorn in the side of the Skinner gang for years, always hanging around trying to wheedle information out of gang members. A thin, dark-haired woman sat opposite Billy. At first glance, the long nose and prominent chin gave her a witch-like appearance, but with the high cheekbones and arched eyebrows, her looks were striking. Greta recognized the dangling amber earrings the woman was wearing. She'd seen her before, but where? Suddenly, it came to her. It was that real estate agent who showed her and Tom around the Harbourfront apartments. What was her name? Dollie? No, Dottie—that was it. What the hell was she doing here?

It was then she noticed the man sitting next to Dottie. His broad back was turned towards Greta, so she couldn't see his face. All Greta could see was the long hair tied in a black leather shoelace, the pinstriped suit. Surely, it couldn't be! As if on cue, the man turned around to signal the server, and Greta saw his face. No doubt about it. It was Rocco. Bittersweet memories came tumbling back. She and Rocco had done it all—wild parties in Montreal, rock-and-roll concerts, and all-night drinking binges. They'd been an item for seven years until he got into cocaine and dumped her for some Russian broad who was addicted to the stuff. The way he casually threw her out still rankled. *No*, thought Greta, *rankled wasn't the right word. It hurt.*

A warrant was out for Rocco's arrest in connection with an armed robbery last month. Here was Greta's chance to get even. A server approached Rocco, and when she saw them talking, Greta grabbed her purse, placed a five-dollar bill on the table, and hurried towards the door. The maitre d' looked surprised, but relieved, as he opened the door for her. "Leaving already, Mrs. Snead?"

"I got better things to do than waste my time on that piece of... garbage."

Greta rushed to the car. The police would be interested in knowing the whereabouts of one Cyril Skinner, better known as Rocco. Her confrontation with Tom would have to wait. She had more important things to do right now. She fumbled in the glove compartment for the cell phone. After a fruitless search, she remembered it was plugged into the electrical outlet in her living room, being recharged. Damn!

Of all the bad luck. She'd have to find a public phone booth to make her 911 call.

***

Greta decided she'd drive to the supermarket a few blocks away and make the phone call from there. It would be too risky making the call from Da Vinci's or anywhere too close, since someone might spot her. She felt a sense of satisfaction as she turned the ignition in the car. She couldn't wait to see the look on Rocco's face when the fuzz turned up!

With her mind on Rocco, Greta reversed out of the parking spot without checking her mirrors. A powerful thud jolted through her body. Glancing into her rearview mirror, she cringed when she saw a yellow Corvette with a huge dent in its side. Oh, shit! A tall blond guy climbed out of the Corvette. A tight fitting white T-shirt and blue jeans revealed a strong muscular body, and as he strode purposefully towards Greta's car, she saw his tanned arms were covered with tattoos. He reminded her a little bit of her boyfriend Antonio, but this stud was better looking.

His dark eyes sparked with anger as he confronted her. "What do you think you're doing, lady! Don't you look in your mirror!"

He had an American accent. Southern. Maybe Texan. Very sexy.

"You can't have been looking where you were going, otherwise you'd have seen me trying to back out!" Greta retorted.

"You weren't just backing out!" he yelled. "You were gunning it!"

By now, several curious onlookers had gathered around to watch the proceedings. Greta decided to change tactics. Her eyes filled with tears. "I've just seen my husband with another woman!" It was somewhat true. "I wasn't thinking straight." That part was definitely true. She leaned forward in her seat, as if in distress. From the corner of her eye, she could see his eyes feast on her cleavage.

He cleared his throat. "I'm Wayne Leverson. From Texas." He held out his hand.

She folded her hand into his. His handshake was firm and strong. "Greta. Greta... Lovejoy." Quick thinking on her part to use her maiden name. The sooner she rid herself of any association with that toad of a husband, the better.

"Perhaps we could discuss this over a drink."

She fumbled for a tissue and dabbed her eyes. "I think that's a very good idea."

"Do you know of a place?"

"Slim Joe's is just around the corner. Has live music and the bartender is a friend of mine. Makes the best martinis in town."

He grinned. "Well, sugar, what are we waiting for? Let's go."

***

This guy's a real hunk, thought Greta, as she sipped her second martini. *Pity he's only in town for a few days, we could have had a real blast. I wonder what he does for a living.*

"Our family ranch has a couple thousand acres. We raise cattle and horses. Ever been to Texas?"

Greta shook herself. Was he a mind reader? "No, but it sounds wonderful." *He's obviously loaded*, she thought.

"I'm up here on business, but I need to get away from the phone sometimes." His eyes wandered all over her. "Especially in the company of a beautiful woman."

The phone! Suddenly, Greta was on her feet. She'd forgotten to phone the police! Now, it was more than likely too late. "I gotta go!" she called back to Wayne as she shot out of the bar and headed towards the public phones.

Four sets of eyes were glued on Rocco. "Now, I'm quite prepared to stay here all night, if needs be." Rocco took out another cigar from his inside pocket and proceeded to light it.

Dottie cleared her throat. "What makes you so sure that one of us has this jewelry you're after?" She'd hoped to sound authoritative, but her voice came out crackly and weak.

"I have my sources," Rocco sneered.

"You're bluffing," Dottie cried.

Rocco's fist slammed down on the table. "I don't bluff, lady." His eyes fell on Billy. "Billy here hasn't got the smarts to be discreet. Didn't you notice you was being followed the other night, Billy?"

Billy swallowed hard. "You mean... Snake?"

"I don't name names. My source tells me you made a phone call. 'I got a buyer for that emerald jewelry,' you said." He took a puff of his cigar, and blew the smoke into Billy's face. Billy had a coughing fit. "'Meet me at Da Vinci's on Thursday at 7,' you said. So, the way I see it, one of you..." He looked around the table. "...has the jewelry. You'd better cough up if you know what's good for you. Just remember, I got this!" And he whipped out the gun from his pocket, just far enough for them to get the message. Everyone sat still, not daring to move.

Suddenly, there were some scuffling noises behind them. The young boy in the booth next to theirs popped his head over the top, his face smeared with ketchup. In a loud voice, he exclaimed, "Look, Dad, that man's got a gun!"

"Get down from there right away, Jimmy!" a man's voice called out.

As suddenly as the small face had appeared, it disappeared. Muffled voices could be heard from the booth. "He has a gun, Dad. I saw it..."

His sister's voice cried out, "I wanna see the gun!"

A woman's high-pitched voice broke in. "Keep your voice down, Jimmy! And June, shut up!" The same voice now took on a different tone. "I've told you, Alfred; Jimmy has an overactive imagination. You gotta talk with him. He's going to get into real trouble one of these days the way he goes on!"

"All right, all right," the man replied impatiently. "Come on, Jimmy." There was more scuffling, and the boy and his father walked around to Dottie's booth.

The man pushed his son in front of him. "My boy's got something to say to you."

The boy looked down at his feet.

"Go on!" urged the father.

"I'm sorry," a very quiet voice said.

"Speak up, Jimmy!" his father urged, but Jimmy said nothing and continued to look at his feet.

"I think the boy got a bit confused." Dottie's heart lurched at the sound of Rocco's gravelly voice. "He saw me pull out this and thought it was a gun." Rocco produced a metal box from his pocket. He opened it and showed the boy the contents. "See. This is where I keep my cigars when I'm travelin' around."

The boy looked at the cigars, and then looked back at Rocco. "I didn't see that box. It was a gun."

Dottie studied Rocco's face. She could see patches of red appear on his cheeks as he stared at the boy. Fortunately, the server appeared at that moment. "Another drink, Rocco honey?"

His eyes still glued on the boy, Rocco shook his head.

"What about your friends here?" The server glanced over the group.

Dottie chirped up. "I'd like another glass of diet ginger ale, please." She figured that if the server was around, nothing too serious could happen. "And a large order of cheese nachos!" Dottie never ate nachos, but they were the first thing that came into her head.

Dottie caught Mabel's eye. "I'd like a diet Pepsi," Mabel said. She looked meaningfully at Billy and Tom. "I think these gentlemen would like something to drink as well."

Tom got the message. "Ginger ale for me."

"Me, too," piped up Billy, his eyes darting nervously around.

The appearance of the server gave Jimmy's father the excuse he needed to escape. "Come on, Jimmy." He hustled the reluctant boy away.

After the server strode off, Dottie held her breath. Now what? Suddenly, out of nowhere, a female voice drawled, "What boulder have you been hiding under?" Dottie turned around. Even in the subdued lighting of the restaurant, there was no mistaking the busty blonde in the tight spandex skirt and revealing top who stared down at Rocco. It was Graciana. "You've put on weight since I saw you, what was it, seven years ago?" she mocked. "Seven years! Who'd a thought it!"

"Greta!" Beads of sweat had formed on Rocco's forehead. For the first time since he'd arrived, he looked nervous. "You're looking good, baby. Tom here must be takin' good care of you." His voice had taken on an ingratiating tone.

"That s.o.b.!" Greta shot a fiery glance at Tom. "He's no better than the rest of you men. You're all cheats and liars!" She turned to Rocco, her eyes full of venom. "When you dumped me for that Russian broad, you figured I'd just go away and nurse a broken heart. But you don't know me." A triumphant smile played on her lips. She raised her hand, and two burly men approached the booth.

One of the men spoke. "Cecil Skinner, I am arresting you on a charge of armed robbery..." The police officer's voice droned on as he read his rights. Rocco's face was like stone. The men grabbed Rocco by the arms and handcuffed him. Greta pushed her face close to Rocco's. "I've waited for a long time to get even with you, Rocco, and I'm gonna savour the moment."

As he was hustled away, Greta turned on Tom. "Thought you'd get away with it, didn't you? Thought you'd sell the jewelry and leave. I got news for you, pal. You ain't got the jewelry no more."
Tom patted his breast pocket. "It's here."

Greta smirked. "Why don't you take a look?"

Tom retrieved a small black pouch from his pocket. He opened it carefully and shook out its contents. A flashy necklace of green stones and matching earrings fell out. He looked closely. "What the...?"

"Don't worry. The real jewelry's in good hands. Antonio and I are leaving tonight."

"Leaving for where?"

Her eyes sparked. "Do you think I'm crazy enough to tell you that? We're going where it's warm. The place we've chosen has the perfect climate, and it's a wonderful place to chill out." With that, she turned and marched towards the door.

For the next few minutes, nobody spoke. Dottie searched in her purse for the cigarillos and lighter, grateful that the restaurant chose to ignore the new law. Once the cigarillo was lit, she inhaled deeply. So much had happened since she and Mabel had walked into the restaurant—first, Tom's arrival, and then Rocco who terrified them all with his threats, and finally, the slinky Greta, who much to everyone's relief, had Rocco arrested.

The server wandered over and asked them if they wanted anything else to drink.

"Looks like you all need double brandies," she remarked, her eyes glancing towards the front door where Rocco had been unceremoniously hustled out. No one responded.

Dottie looked at each of them. "Who'd like coffee?"

"I would," Mabel said.

"Not for me. I'll be on my way." Billy squeezed his way past Tom and, shoulders hunched, exited hastily.

Tom struggled to his feet. "I don't need any coffee, either."

"Not so fast, buster!" Dottie snapped. "You're not going anywhere. You've got a lot of explaining to do."

"I need to use the washroom."

"Don't be long. We'll be waiting."

"So, I guess that'll be just two coffees." The server turned to go. "I'll be right back."

"Greta appears to have had a very colourful life," Dottie commented. "Thank goodness, she recognized Rocco and had him arrested."

"I recognized her voice when we were in *Roos*. It wasn't until I saw her a few minutes ago that I realized why. She was that rude receptionist I told you about at Tom's car dealership."

"That figures."

Mabel rested her chin on the heel of her hand. "How did we get ourselves in this situation, Dottie?" she remarked, her voice flat. "It can't be good for our health."

"What's got into you?"

"What do you mean?"

Dottie smiled affectionately at her friend. "You don't usually let anything get you down."

The server brought their coffee and left some creamers and packets of sugar on the table before rushing off to serve another customer.

"It's that Rocco chap," Mabel confessed as she stirred sweetener into her mug. "He threw me for a loop with his threats. Do you really think he would have used that gun?"

"I get the feeling he's more brawn than brains, but it doesn't take brains to shoot someone." Dottie tapped her fingers impatiently. Where was Tom? She glanced around the restaurant, but there was no sign of him. "Hmm."

Mabel looked at Dottie. "Are you thinking what I'm thinking?"

"Yes, I think our friend has done a bunk. He knows he's going to be given the third degree and will have to answer some very awkward questions." Dottie stood up. "I'm going to have a word with the maitre d'."

Rolando confirmed Dottie's suspicions. "Mr. Snead left— let me see—less than five minutes ago, madam."

Furious, Dottie returned to the booth. "He's gone."

"The chicken! And we can't do anything about it. We don't even know where he lives."

"True, but if he thinks he's going to get away without even an explanation…"

"He won't!" Mabel sat up straight. "We'll pull out all stops. Somehow, we will find him and make him face the music."

CHAPTER 25

Т he next morning, Dottie decided to take out her frustration over Tom's skedaddle by attacking the tall hedge that ran between her garden and the Bottomleys'. It was her least favourite gardening job, but clipping the overgrown foliage suited her mood. Using a stepladder, she started hacking the top of the hedge, figuring she could reach the middle and lower sections from the ground. As she laboured on, sweat trickled her back and legs. She wiped her face with the corner of her cotton top. It was just as well she'd opted for shorts in this muggy heat. Cursing softly under her breath, she lopped the last straggly branches at the top. The chirping of the birds around the feeder mingled with the sharp snap of the clippers as one more branch fell to the ground. At this rate, she'd have the hedge finished in an hour.

An agonized cry pierced the air, and startled birds flew off the feeder in one big whoosh. Dottie jumped, and the ladder wobbled precariously as she struggled to regain her balance. Taking a deep breath to calm her racing heart, she peered over the shorn hedge. Her eyes darted around her neighbour's garden. All appeared to be serene and peaceful.

Then, out of the corner of her eye, Dottie saw something move. When she turned to look, an uncomfortable tingle crept down her spine. The sliding door that led from the deck into the bungalow was wide open, and a flimsy white curtain, lifted by the breeze, billowed through a gaping hole in the screen door. Dottie scrambled down the ladder and ran across the lawn to the bungalow. After a quick glance around, she stepped through the slashed screen into the Bottomleys' den.

Larry lay sprawled on the floor, blood oozing from a gash in his forehead. She bent over the inert body to look closer. His eyes were closed, face sunken and pale. Dottie feared the worst, until she noticed a piece of fluff near his nose fluttering back and forth. He was breathing, thank God.

A hysterical voice cried out, "What have you done!"

The clippers fell out of Dottie's hand onto the hardwood floor. She spun around to find Gert standing in the doorway, a look of horror on her face. Gert rushed across the room. Bending over Larry, she touched his face. "He's not breathing! You've killed him. You've killed my Larry!"

"Gert, listen to me," Dottie pleaded. "Larry's alive. I'm going to call the ambulance. Cover him with that blanket on the sofa. OK?"

Dottie picked up the phone and dialled 911. She was glad to hear the reassuring voice of the operator and passed on the details to her. "How long will the ambulance be?"

"There's been a big accident on the QEW. We'll be there as soon as possible, ma'am."

Her heart sank. "I see." Dottie hung up the phone. She turned around to find Gert clutching the blanket, her eyes staring into space. "Let me help you," Dottie offered, taking it away from her.

As Dottie pulled the mohair blanket over Larry, Gert screamed out, "Get away from him!" In one swoop, she grabbed the hedge clippers off the floor and moved towards Dottie, her eyes full of hate. "I've seen you trying to seduce him with those short skirts and high heels." Gert's venomous rant filled the air. "Don't think I haven't noticed. I know what you're up to." An ice-cold spike of fear shot through Dottie as Gert came closer, the blades of the clippers glinting. "You thought you'd try it on again today, didn't you? You made sure that Larry was by himself, and then you waltzed over in those shorts."

Dottie slowly backed away but kept talking. "Gert, someone broke into your bungalow today and attacked Larry. I heard a cry and came over to check." She willed herself to keep calm. "The ambulance men will be here at any moment. Why don't you put those clippers down and sit with Larry until they arrive."

As though she hadn't heard a word Dottie said, Gert rambled on. "People like you take advantage of Larry. They make fun of him; they think he doesn't have any brains. They don't know him as I do. That George Fernandes was always making snide remarks. He told his friends that Larry was retarded. Retarded! Well, I showed him! He wasn't going to get away with making fun of my Larry. When I saw that toad in the casino, I saw my chance to get back at him."

Dottie's mouth went dry. "What do you mean you saw your chance to get back at him?"

"What do you think I mean?" Gert sneered. "Get rid of him, of course. Anyone who messes around with my Larry must answer to me!"

Dottie felt sick. "Are you saying you killed George?"

"I knew George liked gambling, and I'd seen him at the casino before." Her eyes gleamed. "I always carried a knife with me, just in case."

"How do you get past security?"

"Easy. I carry an umbrella. It's a perfect fit for my knife."

Dottie's heart was beating so hard she felt sure that Gert could hear. "So, you were looking for an opportunity to kill him?"

Gert stared into the distance. "It was easy. George was standing by your machine. When the lights started to flash, I knew you'd won a jackpot. With all the fuss that goes with winning, I managed to get right behind him. By the time people had moved away, George was lying on the ground with a knife in his back."

Dottie felt bile rise into her throat. "Why are you telling me this?"

"You won't live to tell the tale!" A hideous grin crossed her face. "It doesn't matter that you know."

With the clippers pointing at Dottie, she lunged forward. Dottie jumped to one side, and the clippers stabbed into the sofa. She tried to get away, but Gert pushed her onto the sofa and grabbed her around the throat. Before Gert could exert any pressure, Dottie screamed at the top of her voice.

Gert's strong fingers pressed into Dottie's neck. "You think anyone will hear you?" she mocked. "By the time you're found, it will be too late."

Gert's fingers pressed harder. Everything started to go black. Just as Dottie thought she was going to die, someone leapt through the broken screen, ran across the room, and yanked Gert away. "My God, Dottie," a familiar voice rang out. "What's going on?"

"Fred!" Dottie rasped, rubbing her neck.

He held the struggling Gert. "Are you okay, Dottie?"

"I will be in a minute." She took some deep breaths. "What are you doing here?"

"I called to see you. I was about to ring the doorbell when I heard a scream."

"Thank God you were around." Dottie climbed off the sofa. "I'll call the police. The ambulance is already on its way."

***

Later, after Larry was taken to the hospital and Gert was taken to headquarters for questioning, Fred prepared

Dottie a hot toddy. "It's got lemon and honey in it," he explained. "Good for the throat."

Dottie lay on her living room sofa with Muggins beside her. She sipped the hot drink. "So, why **did** you call around today?" She had negative feelings about Fred since their last encounter and hadn't expected to see him again, ever.

He cleared his throat. "It's very simple. You lent me $1,000 a while ago, and I wanted to return it." He fished in his jacket pocket, produced an envelope, and handed it to her. A smile played on his lips. "There's only one catch."

Oh, here we go, it's never straightforward with Fred. "What do you mean—a catch?"

"I'd like to take you out for lunch. That is, if your fiancé doesn't mind. This time, I won't be asking for any favours, I promise."

"My fiancé?"

"I think you said his name is Jim."

Oh, shoot! Dottie felt her face heat up.

Fred grinned. "Or have you split up?" He leaned towards her and kissed the top of her head. "I've told you before, Dottie, you're a poor liar."

Dottie couldn't think of anything to say.

"So. Are we for lunch or what?"

Dottie smiled. "As you've saved my life, Fred, I think I owe you that much."

CHAPTER 26

Dottie was about to take another bite of whole-wheat toast when she saw the headline, "Port Dover Expecting over 100,000 Bikers on Friday the Thirteenth." That was next week! Brushing away the crumbs, she smoothed out the paper to catch every word.

Ever since Tom gave her the Harley, Dottie had spent hours roaring down highways and zigzagging along country roads. Her driving skills had improved along with her self confidence. What a great experience it would be to drive to Port Dover and meet other bike owners!

She wished Mabel would come with her. So far, she hadn't been able to persuade her friend to climb on the back and go for a spin. "You won't get me on a motorbike," Mabel had declared. "My brother Giles had a bad accident on one in his teens. Those things scare me to death."

As she cleared away breakfast dishes, Dottie racked her brains. What argument could she use that might encourage Mabel to at least try it? She remembered when Tom had presented her with the bike. How gorgeous he'd looked in his leather gear! She and Mabel had been taken in by his charm, and he'd been conning them all along. They hadn't set eyes on him since the day he escaped from the restaurant. A thought popped into her head. Tom was an avid biker. What if he and his friends decided to go to Port Dover on the thirteenth? She rushed to the phone. "Mabel, Can I drop around for a few minutes?" *Play it cool,* she reminded herself. "I'd like to run something past you."

"I'm meeting my bridge group in an hour."

"This won't take long."

"All right. I'll see you in a few minutes."

***

Mabel's eyes sparked. "I've told you, Dottie, I don't want to ride that bike. Why won't you take no for an answer!"

"The thing is I wouldn't ask you under normal circumstances, but there's a bike fest in Port Dover." Dottie gave Mabel the details.

"So, not one noisy motorcycle, but one hundred thousand. And I'm supposed to want to go because?"

"What if Tom's there?"

"What makes you think that? Has he been in touch with you?"

"No, nothing like that. The thing is he's really into bikes, and this Port Dover thing is big."

"And you think any biker worth his salt will be there on Friday."

"For sure."

Mabel replied in a flat voice. "You want me to be a passenger on that bike, so we can go to Port Dover and find Tom."

Dottie chose her words carefully. "I can go by myself, but it won't be easy. If you come with me, we'd have a much better chance of finding him."

Mabel checked her watch. "I've got to leave." She looked at Dottie. "Just one thing."

"What?"

"Do you have a helmet for me."

Dottie gave Mabel a big hug. "Not only do I have a helmet, I've had a new seat and passenger backrest fitted, so it's extra comfortable."

"I'll be the judge of that."

***

Friday the thirteenth dawned bright and sunny. Determined to reach Port Dover in lots of time to find a parking space, Dottie picked up Mabel at 6:30 a.m.

Mabel yawned as she closed the front door. "This is much too early for me. I don't get up until eight as a rule." She looked at Dottie. "What a splendid leather outfit you're wearing." She perused her own hot pink jacket, lime green top, and multi-coloured cotton pants. "This is a bit casual, I'm afraid."

Mabel's outrageous colour scheme would fit right in. "Don't worry. I've been to a couple of smaller events like this. People wear all kinds of clothing—you won't feel out of place."

Mabel's eyes darted over the cobalt blue bike. "So, this is the monster."

Dottie clipped on her helmet and helped Mabel with hers. After Mabel had settled in the passenger seat, Dottie climbed on the bike and turned on the ignition. She glanced around at Mabel who looked as if she were about to be driven to her own execution. "Are you ready?" she shouted over the roar of the engine.

"As ready as I'll ever be!"

With all the stopping at traffic lights, turning corners, and slowing down, the early part of the journey was a bit rough for someone who'd never ridden a motorbike. Dottie hoped that Mabel wasn't put off, but once they reached Highway 403, the journey became smoother. If traffic wasn't too heavy, they should make Port Dover in plenty of time. Before merging onto Route 6, Dottie decided it was time for a pit stop. She pulled off the highway and found a

Tim Hortons coffee shop. "Well," she asked as they removed their helmets, "what do you think?"

"I never thought I'd say this," Mabel replied, "but I can't remember the last time I had such fun!"

Dottie smiled. "I'm pleased you feel that way. I knew you would once you tried it."

"One of these days, I'll get you to go white-water rafting. Once you try it..."

"OK, OK, we'll see."

***

As they neared their destination, traffic slowed, and Dottie found herself behind a stream of motorbikes. At last, a sign for Port Dover came into view, and they drove into the little town. It was already filling up. Bikers milled around, chatting and smoking.

"Let's find a restaurant," Mabel said. "All that fresh air has given me an appetite."

Feeling peckish as well, Dottie eased into a parking space near a café and turned off the ignition. As she reached to unclip her helmet, Mabel tapped her on the shoulder.

"There he is!" Mabel hissed. "There's Tom!"

Dottie turned around. Obviously, this was her lucky day! She'd been concerned that, with a hundred thousand bikers in town, Tom might be difficult to spot. Yet here he was, the very first person they'd run into. Clad in black leather, Tom was sitting astride his bike in front of the café, chatting with a curvaceous blonde.

"Typical!" Mabel remarked. "I wonder what stories he's telling her!"

"We have to plan our strategy, Mabel. If we rush over, he'll see us, and we might lose the opportunity. I think we should walk casually towards him..." The roar of an engine drowned her voice. All heads turned to watch a Yamaha charge down the road before turning onto a side street. Dottie glanced around. Her eyes met Tom's. For a few seconds, he froze, and then reached for his helmet. "Let's go, Mabel!" Dottie cried. "He's seen us!"

After slamming on the helmet, Tom turned on the ignition. Traffic clogged the street, but a considerate biker allowed Tom to pull in front of him. Dottie wasn't so fortunate. Biting her lip, she could see Tom's bike moving farther away by the minute.

The snake of bikes eased up, and for a few moments, the road was clear. Dottie revved the engine, pulled on her goggles, and eased onto Main Street.

The police were out in force, directing traffic. The bike crawled along. Dottie could feel the sweat trickling down her back as the sun's rays burned into the leather. She should have opted for her new lightweight mesh jacket, instead of worrying about looking "splendid" as Mabel put it.

On her left, a group of young women in skin-tight tees, tattoos engraved on their arms, busily chatted with guys wearing bandanas around their heads. The men's outfits were a mixture of jean jackets, colourful shirts, and T-shirts with various insignias; the women's outfits were similar, but some sported bikini tops, tight-fitting jeans, sleeveless leather zip-up vests, and shorts. Mixed in with the motley collection of outfits were a few slinky leather jackets and chaps.

Dottie felt a poke in the ribs. "Look to your right!" Mabel shouted. A small crowd had gathered around a man wearing an orange thong and nothing else. As if on cue, Dottie spotted a man standing in an upstairs window, nude from the waist up, with a live snake curled around his neck.

Despite all the distractions, Dottie didn't let Tom's black Harley out of sight. He was several bikes ahead, until they came to a crossroads, where he turned left. Dottie's heart sank. She'd never catch him now. Then, she got a break when the traffic ahead began to speed up. Signalling left, she followed Tom. The street was long and straight, but there was no sign of him.

There was always an off chance that Tom's bike would run into mechanical problems, and they'd find him sitting at the side of the road, looking for help. This thought, however far-fetched, spurred her on. Now, the road began to wind, and as she took a curve, she saw a flash of metal. She breathed a sigh of relief when Tom's bike came into view. All was not lost!

The road curved over a railway track, cutting through rock-strewn undergrowth and marshes. An archway of trees, their branches heavy with leaves, created alternating light and shade, making it difficult to see. Tom disappeared for a while, but when she caught sight of him again, Dottie accelerated.

Dottie was right behind Tom when his bike hit a large boulder. She watched in horror as the bike spun out of control, flinging him into the air like a rag doll.

CHAPTER 27

Slamming on the brakes, Dottie skidded to a halt close to the boulder. The two women climbed off the bike and looked around, expecting to find Tom lying in the undergrowth.

"Tom, it's Mabel, can you hear me?"

"He can't hear you if he's been knocked out," Dottie snapped. Despite her anger towards Tom, cold fear gripped her heart. Would they find him badly injured or worse? They spent the next few minutes searching through the undergrowth, but there was no sign of him.

Mabel grabbed Dottie's arm. "I think I heard something."

They fell silent, straining to listen. Everything was quiet, except for a few chirping birds and rustling in the leaves.

"Help! Help! Over here!"

They whipped around and saw Tom a short distance away, standing in a pond. As they got closer, they could see pieces of algae hanging from his helmet and bits of mud and dead insects stuck on his face. His sleek leather jacket was a mess of green slime.

"Dottie, Mabel," he pleaded. "Can you help me get out of this pond? My feet are stuck in the mud!"

Mabel was about to rush over when Dottie grabbed her arm. "Don't be in too much of a hurry," she hissed. "We've got him cornered. Let's make the most of it."

Mabel protested. "We can't leave him like that!"

"Once we get him out, he'll probably escape again—if his bike's still working."

"You're right." Mabel tapped her lips with an index finger.

"What are you two beautiful ladies talking about?" Once you rescue me, I'll take you out for an elegant dinner…"

"No way!" they replied in unison.

"Well, we could start with coffee," Tom continued. "There's a small diner nearby."

"Okay, I know what we'll do," Mabel whispered. "If Tom's bike is working, I'll ride to the restaurant as his passenger."

"You'll what!"

"He wouldn't dare to harm me after all that's happened."

Dottie thought about Mabel's plan. Tom was a thief and con artist, but unlikely a kidnapper.

They grabbed his arms to yank him out of the pond, but the mud gripped his legs. With one final pull, they heaved him onto the bank. Black mud clung to his boots and the legs of his jeans from his thighs down. Using grass, they helped him remove the worst of the algae and muck. Dottie had a good supply of Handiwipes, so he was able to clean his hands and face.

"You'll do for now." She paused. "You'd better check your bike." Tom examined the chrome and paintwork. "I can't see any major damage apart from a few dents." When he turned on the ignition, the engine roared into life.

"OK," Dottie said, "we'll have coffee in that restaurant you spoke about. Mabel is going to be your passenger, and I'll be following right behind you, so no shenanigans. Let's go," Dottie ordered. "Mabel's new to this, so don't drive too fast."

With a grin, Mabel climbed behind Tom and strapped on her helmet. *She thinks this is an adventure,* Dottie mused. *Let's hope it doesn't turn nasty.*

* * *

When they arrived at the restaurant, Tom wanted to go to the washroom to get rid of some lingering pieces of algae.

"We'll sit here and wait for you," Dottie said, pointing to a table close to the washroom. She checked her watch. "If you aren't out of there in five minutes, I'll como and get you."

"You wouldn't go into a men's washroom." He studied her face. "Yes, you probably would." He was back in three minutes flat.

Dottie pushed a cup of black coffee towards him. Folding her arms, she looked Tom right in the eye. "You've got a lot of explaining to do. And we're in no hurry."

He gulped down half his coffee before he looked at the two women. "My dear Dottie and Mabel." He extended his arms and inclined his head to one side. "How can I begin to say how sorry I am for the way I treated you!"

Dottie felt her blood pressure rise. "Don't you 'dear Dottie' me with your fake accent and European charm! Where exactly are you from?"

Looking defeated, Tom cleared his throat. "I was born in Montreal, but my parents came to Canada from Europe. My mother was Italian, and my father was Spanish."

"You lied about your name and your so-called niece." Dottie couldn't resist a touch of sarcasm. "It's amazing how your niece, Graciana, morphed into your wife Greta."

Tom fiddled with his coffee spoon. "Greta and me... we found out you were in real estate. That's why I contacted you to find an apartment."

"Which you had no intention of buying!" Dottie glared. "You thought it was a good way to find out about the jewelry."

"Looking for an apartment was genuine. Greta wanted to move into the city."

"What about telling me your name was Vincenzo," Mabel butted in, "and that you owned a car dealership!"

"I did own the car dealership," Tom insisted. "I sold it shortly after I found that Lotus Elise for you."

"And do you really know an international jewelry appraiser?"

"Yes."

Mabel pursed her lips. "Hmm."

"Your business card says you are a jewelry appraiser," Dottie said.

"I worked in my uncle's jewelry business in Montreal for many years. I know a fair amount about gems, but an appraisal of that magnitude needed a real expert."

"Why should we believe you?" Dottie asked.

"Perhaps if I tell you what happened, it might convince you."

He looks as if he's about to cry, she thought. *He's a good actor; I'll give him that.* "Go on."

"About two months ago, I found out George Fernandes was planning a job that involved some antique diamond and emerald jewelry worth millions. My contact also told me the date of the heist." He paused. "After the robbery took place, I followed them to the casino. I didn't know which of them was carrying the jewelry, until I saw George slip an envelope into your pocket, Dottie."

Dottie looked at Tom over the rim of her coffee cup. "So, if you saw that, you must have seen who killed him."

"No, I just saw the lights flash on your machine and the crowd of people."

"There's one thing I can't figure out. Why did you bother to make copies of the jewelry? Why go to all that trouble? When I gave you the jewelry, you could have just taken it and escaped to some warm island somewhere."

"That was because of you."

When Tom smiled, she glared. "Don't try to get around me, Tom."

"I'm not. It's just that you remind me of someone I knew long ago in Montreal."

"Another of your victims, I suppose," Dottie scoffed.

"She was the love of my life." A faraway look came into his eyes. "I met her in acting school. Once we graduated, she went to London, and we lost touch."

"Acting school! That figures!"

"So, where do I come in?" Mabel piped up.

"I can answer that," said Dottie. "Because we weren't speaking to each other, it was easier for him to get away with playing dual roles. And then, I was away for four weeks looking fter my grandchildren in Unionville."

"Still," Mabel persisted, her eyes glued on Tom. "You knew I didn't have the emeralds."

"I daresay he found out you were a widow of substantial means with antiques or jewelry lying around your house that he could sell for a nice profit," Dottie said. She turned to Tom. "I'm right, aren't I?"

Tom nodded. He drained his coffee cup and looked at Mabel. "Those paintings you own are worth a packet. The antique jewelry I had appraised for you was worth a lot of money, even more than I'd imagined."

"Why did you bring it back? You could have stolen it." Mabel broke in. "I suppose you're going to tell me I remind you of your mother."

"But that's exactly what happened. You are so kind and sympathetic. Just like my mother, God rest her soul. In the end, I couldn't go through with it."

Dottie still had questions. "What about you and Billy? When I told you I'd seen you talking with him at the stables, you said you were making a deal for the Harley-Davidson. When I thanked Billy for it, he had no idea what I was talking about." Dottie took a deep breath. "You might as well come clean, Tom. I found boxes of jewelry and cases of wine hidden in Yolanda's loft."

"That's where he and Den keep their stuff until it's cooled off. They've used the loft for years, but they're mostly small time. It's not my gig."

The three of them fell silent for a few minutes while the server brought around the coffee carafe and refilled their cups. Dottie broke the silence. "Did Greta go away with Antonio?"

"Oh, yes, Antonio has plenty of money. He'll be able to keep her in the lifestyle she's always wanted."

"You don't seem to mind," Mabel observed.

"I've waited for this moment for a long time," Tom answered simply. "Greta's a very demanding woman. And she has a terrible temper."

Mabel leaned forward. "That night you came to my house..."

"When I arrived home after I'd dropped you off, Greta was waiting for me. We had a big fight, and she threw a vase at me."

"So, that's how you got the cut on your eye. Why did you come to my house?"

"I was feeling sorry for myself. You are so kind-hearted, Mabel, and I felt the need to be…"

"Mothered."

"I suppose that was it, yes."

They fell silent for a while.

"What are you going to do now that Greta has the jewelry?" Mabel asked.

"It's best you don't know." He smiled. "Right now, we are going to eat, and I'll tell you about a proposition I have for you." He turned and beckoned to the server who came to their table. "We would like to have menus, please. And a litre of your house wine."

"We have a Merlot or a Shiraz, or would you prefer white? Our white house wine is a Chardonnay."

"Ladies?"

Dottie shrugged. "Either is fine with me."

"I prefer Chardonnay, if you don't mind," Mabel said.

"Then, Chardonnay it is! Now, let's see what's on the menu."

This, thought Dottie, was the old Tom—Enrique, Vincenzo, whoever—charming, attentive, and genial. Oddly, some of her anger towards him had dissipated. She would even go so far as to say she was quite fond of him in a strange sort of way, but she would never let him or anyone else know that.

The three of them chose the lunch special—grilled salmon with a garden salad. Hunger pangs hit Dottie as the server placed the food in front of her, and she ate with enthusiasm. "So what's the proposition you were going to make?" she said between mouthfuls of fish.

Tom leaned towards them. "How do you fancy a holiday in France and Italy next summer—Provence and Tuscany, to be precise."

The women stared at him. "What's the catch?" asked Mabel.

"No catch, I promise." He smiled. "I have a small house in Provence near Avignon. An aunt left it to me. It is an old stone house in a tiny hamlet called St. Jerome. There is a small grocery store and a bar, that's all. The house is decorated in Provençal style, with all the mod cons."

Dottie stared at Tom. "Why are you doing this?"

His voice softened. "It is my way of saying how sorry I am for causing you distress. In addition to my house in Provence, a friend of mine owns an olive farm in Tuscany near Siena. I borrow it from time to time, whenever I am in Europe."

As Tom described the farm set in the Tuscan hillside, Dottie felt her excitement grow. What a wonderful chance to have a holiday like that! Then, she thought of the old saying that Mabel was fond of quoting, if something seems too good to be true, it probably is. "You expect us to trust you after everything that's happened?"

"You have a very good point." Tom sipped his coffee thoughtfully.

Mabel's eyes were sparkling. "It all sounds..."

Dottie pressed hard on Mabel's foot. "What Mabel is about to say is that it sounds very nice, but we can't go. We've been invited to stay at a friend's cottage on Lake Muskoka next summer."

From the corner of her eye, Dottie saw Mabel look at her in shock.

"Right now, we're going home. It's been a very long day." Dottie stood up. "Come on, Mabel."

"Before you go, here is my business card." He handed a gold-embossed card to Dottie. "My real business card," he added. "If your other plans fall through, and you'd like to take me up on my offer, call me."

Dottie examined the card. Tom's name was engraved in copperplate. Beneath his name, the caption read "Antique Dealer. Specialist in jewelry and classic cars."

***

Once they were outside, Mabel turned on Dottie. "I can't believe you would refuse an offer like that! Just imagine, driving through the French countryside, then the Tuscan scenery... And what's this nonsense about going to stay on Lake Muskoka next year. We don't even know anyone in that area, except my niece Yolanda, of course. And she won't be at her cottage next summer because she and Arnold are going to Europe."

"Mabel!" Dottie's voice was sharp. "Of course, we aren't going."

Mabel looked at Dottie in amazement. "But you told Tom." A slow smile crossed Mabel's face. "What are you up to, Dottie Flowers?"

"This might be the chance of a lifetime. On the other hand, knowing Tom's character, it could be a big hoax."

"So, what do you propose we do about it?"

"We need to get more details and make sure that he isn't making the whole thing up. He doesn't have a great track record for honesty." She gave Mabel a knowing smile. "We've got to be a bit cautious, that's all. If we play our cards right, we could be driving through France and Italy next summer!"

"How's your French?"

"A lot better than my Italian. If this works out, we'd better sign up for Italian and French lessons at night school!"

209

"Muggins! Muggins!" Dottie tutted with exasperation. Where was he hiding this time? It was 10 p.m., long past his suppertime. She opened a pouch of salmon-flavoured cat food and shook it into his dish. Within minutes, the catch on the kitchen door clicked, and the cat strutted in, tail in air. He hated being cooped up in the house. Most of his days were spent hidden in some dark space, under her bed, inside a closet, or in the broom cupboard. The rest of the time he sat by the sunroom window, tail flicking back and forth, watching for mice and birds.

Dottie yawned. It had been a long day at the office. The idea of curling up in bed with the latest Elizabeth George mystery spurred her on. She checked the front and back doors, made sure all lights were switched off, and headed for bed. As she walked into the dark bedroom, a light flickered across the window. Curious, Dottie crossed the room and peered out. The beam of a flashlight danced over the lawn. She strained to see who it was, but it was too dark. What was he—or she—up to? A terrible thought struck her. What if it was the cat killer?

Dottie pulled on a dark sweater and slacks and rammed on a pair of loafers. She rushed down the stairs. Grabbing a flashlight, she opened the back door and crept outside. Not a leaf stirred in the darkness. She stood by the door, shivering in the chilly night air. A rustle in the hedge made her jump, but it was only a raccoon scurrying across the lawn. She waited. A light moved in the bushes in the garden to the right of her. The intruder was in Margaret's garden.

Margaret's cat, Tiddles, like Muggins, preferred to be outdoors. Despite Margaret's attempts to keep him indoors at night, he sometimes escaped. Dottie prayed that tonight he was sleeping peacefully in his basket.

Creeping along the hedge, she reached the little gate leading into Margaret's garden and peered through one of its slats. It took a while for her eyes to adjust to the dark. Once they did, she could make out the outlines of trees and bushes. The grass crunched, and someone inside the garden crept passed the gate. He—or she—was dressed in black and wearing a facemask. Heart pounding, Dottie remembered that there was a gap in the hedge near the bottom of the garden. She race-walked to it and peeked through. Something soft brushed her face, and she almost shrieked out. Biting her lip, she took another peek. The intruder was half kneeling against the hedge a mere three feet away. From his stance, he appeared to be watching Margaret's bungalow. Here was her chance! Taking a deep breath, she dashed through the gap, lifted her flashlight with two hands, and smashed it down on the intruder's head.

The force of the attack made Dottie lose balance, and she fell backwards. She struggled to her feet. A solitary leaf fluttered over the prone figure that lay on the grass. For one dreadful moment, Dottie wondered if she'd overdone it.

A sigh of relief escaped her lips when she heard a low moan. She bent down and removed the facemask. Her mouth dropped open. "Tom!"

"Dottie, is that you?" he groaned.

'What are you doing here, sneaking around in the dark with a flashlight and dressed like... like Zorro!'

"What about you? Do you make a habit of knocking people on the head with a flashlight?" Tom rubbed the back of his head.

"I saw a beam of light and thought it might be the cat killer."

"Keep your voice down," Tom hissed. "He might hear us."

"Who?"

He sat up. "The cat killer. It's a long story..."

"I bet it is. Give me the *Reader's Digest* version."

"I'm trying to catch the cat killer."

"I gathered that. Have you seen him? I mean is he around here?"

"I think so. I followed him, but he seems to have disappeared."

"Look, we'd better..."

Suddenly, a voice called across the lawn. "Here, pussycat. Here, pussycat!"

The light from Margaret's porch revealed a straggly-haired youth in baggy jeans. Knees bent, he held out a bowl with a fish tail hanging over the side. Dottie shuddered as she remembered that dead cat she'd found in her garden with a fish tail hanging out of his mouth.

"Here, pussycat! Here, pussycat!"

Suddenly, Tiddles ran out of some bushes towards the young man. "That's Margaret's cat!" Dottie whispered.

Tom jumped up and bounded across the lawn. He grabbed the youth. They struggled, but it was clear the young man was stronger and fitter than Tom. He broke free and sprinted away. As he ran past Dottie, she stuck out her foot. He tripped and fell into the ashes of a long dead garden fire. Covered in ash, he tried to stand, but Tom leapt forward and pulled the youth's arm behind his back in an armlock.

"What are you doing?" the youth protested. "Let me go!"

"No way. That's the last cat you'll poison."

"Poison? What are you talking about?"

"You heard me."

"You're making a big mistake!" the young man protested.

"Look in my knapsack, Dottie!" Tom yelled. "There's some tape in there."

While he taped the youth's wrists and ankles, Dottie used Tom's cell phone to call the police. "They're on their way!" she shouted.

"I'll go to the front of the house and watch out for them," Tom said.

When he left, the young man spoke. "Look, you've got the wrong guy. I came out to entice Auntie Margaret's cat into the house. She warned me that he likes to roam around the neighbourhood at night. The next thing, I'm being accused of trying to poison…"

"Did you say 'Auntie Margaret'?" Dottie cut in.

"Yes, she asked me if I wanted to stay in her house for a few days while she visited some friends in Niagara-on-the-Lake and take care of her new cat. I forgot the cat's name."

Dottie looked at the boy. "Speaking of names, what's yours?"

"Simon."

Dottie sighed inwardly. She had heard Margaret speak of her nephew Simon on several occasions. She found Tom and told him. "Oh, crap," he said.

While they removed the tape from Simon's wrists and ankles, Dottie and Tom took turns explaining everything.

"So, you thought I was a cat killer?" To their relief, he grinned. He stood up and shook himself. "What a story I'll have to tell my friends. They'll never believe me!"

A rustling in the bushes at the foot of the garden startled them. Probably raccoons, Dottie mused. She glanced across the lawn as a shadowy figure dashed out from behind a bush.

"Quick," "Tom yelled. "Let's go. That might be our cat killer!"

At that moment, sirens wailed as police cars raced down the street, screeching to a halt outside Margaret's house. "Simon, you go with Tom," Dottie urged. "I'll wait for the police."

"Will do!" Simon agreed.

Dottie sighed. How was she going to get herself out of this one?

***

Dottie had just finished telling the police what had happened when her cell phone rang. It was Tom. "Dottie, we've caught him."

"That's great." She passed the phone over to a police officer. "You need to deal with this."

Within minutes, the police had left, sirens blaring, to pick up the cat killer.

***

After feeding Tiddles, Dottie wandered back to her bungalow. She should be happy and relieved that the cat killer had been found. Now, Muggins could roam outside to his heart's content. Instead, she felt a bit left out of things.

As she reached her bungalow, she saw Tom sitting on the deck steps. "What are you doing here?" Tom threw a half-smoked cigarette on the ground and squished it under his foot.Before Tom had a chance to respond, Dottie cut in, "You're a smoker?"

"I used to smoke two packs a day. Now, I only smoke when I'm under stress."

To think of all the times she'd tried to hide her smoking habit from him! "You're full of surprises."

"Yeah, well." His shoulders sagged.

"Let's go inside. I'll make some coffee. I have something to tell you as well.

***

Dottie carried the mugs of coffee into the living room and handed one to Tom.

"You first."

"What? Oh, yes, the cat killer. Well…"

Dottie interrupted him. "You and Simon caught the cat killer. Why didn't you wait until the police arrived?"

Tom sipped his coffee. "The police and me, we don't see eye-to-eye."

"You're afraid they'd ask too many questions."

"That's about it, yes."

"Okay, I can see that." She propped her feet on a footstool. "So, tell me about the cat killer."

"He does occasional work for the Skinner gang."

"He told you just like that?"

"They hired him to put a dead cat on the Bottomleys' lawn, except he put it on your lawn by mistake. Larry Bottomley had threatened to spill the beans about some job the gang had planned and tried to blackmail them. A dead cat is the gang's way of warning someone to back off or else."

"That's why the skull and crossbones insignia was on the cat's fur."

"Yes."

"I remember wondering why Larry seemed so upset when I told him about the cat on my lawn. Now, I know." Dottie pulled out a packet of cigarillos. "Want one?"

"No, thanks, I'll have one of mine in a minute."

"So, why did this man go on a killing rampage?"

"When he was given the job of leaving a dead cat on Larry's lawn, he got the idea into his head it was a great way to get back at his 'enemies.' His words, not mine. Seems he used to deliver pizza. Some customers gave him a hard time by refusing to pay, saying he was late with delivery. Some even ordered pizza, and when he delivered it, they told him no one had ordered any. Stuff like that. Anyway, he decided to take revenge by poisoning their cats. He liked dogs. He wouldn't kill dogs."

"So, he went around killing all those animals to punish those who 'wronged' him. What a sick individual."

Tom lit a cigarette and took a long drag. "You said you had something to tell me."

"It's about the jewelry."

"Oh?"

"Greta doesn't have the real jewelry."

Tom stared at Dottie. "What are you talking about?"

Dottie explained what happened. "I was so caught up with getting Muggins back safe and sound that I grabbed the wrong envelope."

"And gave it to Charlie."

"Yes, how do you suppose Greta will react when she finds out?"

Folding his hands behind his head, Tom leaned back in the armchair and stretched out his legs. A satisfied smile flickered on his lips. "Put it this way. I'm glad I won't be around. When she gets into one of her tempers, it's not a pretty sight." He touched the red mark under his eye. "I wouldn't want to be in Antonio's shoes."

They smoked in companionable silence. When they'd finished, Tom stood up and stretched. "I must go. Thanks for the coffee."

As Dottie saw him to the door, she came to a decision. "Tom, about the offer of your house in Provence and your friend's farm in Tuscany…"

"Don't apologize. I know you've already made plans for next year." He shook his head. "It's too bad. It's a charming area of France. And Tuscany is beautiful."

"No. I mean, we can go after all."

"You mean… you're taking me up on my offer?"

"That's right. I know I speak for Mabel as well."

He kissed her lightly on the cheek. "That's good news. You won't be sorry."

As Dottie closed the door, her smile faded a bit. As pleased as she was about the prospect of a holiday in France and Italy next summer, she still had misgivings about Tom. He'd pretended to be someone else, had seriously considered stealing jewelry off her and Mabel, and made his living making shady deals with unsavoury individuals such as Billy. Still, she wasn't going to waste her time second-guessing her decision. What was it that Mabel was fond of saying? Let the chips fall where they may.

About the Author

Originally from North Wales, Sheila Gale immigrated to Canada where she worked as a college professor teaching communications courses. Now pursuing a writing career, she has published several short stories, one of which, *Vintage Vampire,* is based on a prize-winning speech she gave at a Toastmasters Club. She is currently working on the third novel of the Dottie Flowers series.

Did you like this book?

If you enjoyed this book, you will find more interesting books at
www.CrystalDreamsPublishing.com

Please take the time to let us know how you liked this book.
Even short reviews of 2-3 sentences can be helpful and may
be used in our marketing materials.

If you take the time to post a review for this book on Amazon.
com, let us know when the review is posted and you will
receive a free audiobook or ebook from our catalog. Simply
email the link to the review once it is live on Amazon.com,
your name, and your mailing address -- send the email to
orders@mmpubs.com with the subject line "Book Review
Posted on Amazon."

If you have questions about this book, our customer loyalty
program, or our review rewards program, please contact us
at info@mmpubs.com.

cdp
CRYSTAL DREAMS
publishing

a division of Multi-Media Publications Inc.

Terror in Manhattan

By Ross L. Barber

Jayne Keener is a young, single all-American girl who, like so many newcomers to the world of Cyberspace, finds herself drawn into the shadowy world of cybersex and adult chat rooms. Following the murder of a suave, mysterious Englishman she has met in a Manhattan bar, Jayne finds herself sucked ever deeper into the subculture of Internet chat rooms.

It is in one such room that she encounters Phillip H. Dreedle; professional hacker, convicted rapist and stalker. Suddenly, Jayne's once sane life is turned on its head, and not even her closest friends are what they seem.

ISBN-13:9781591460404

The Hornbrook Prophecy

By Robert Wickes

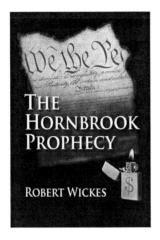

What would happen if the United States government suddenly went bankrupt?

An ancient beheading and a 200-year-old prediction foretell the inevitable consequences of blind ambition and the abuse of power in a thought-provoking, passionate challenge to conventional political wisdom. Maverick Senator Henley Hornbrook fights against unscrupulous President Winston Dillard while a nationwide tax revolt plunges the

country into chaos before Hornbrook unveils a stunning plan that will forever change the nation and preserve its destiny.

Is it fiction, or prediction? In a classic confrontation between government oppression and rugged individualism, The Hornbrook Prophecy will spark debate from the classroom to the bar room about a new, principled hero who fights for more than the girl and the gold.

ISBN-13:9781591463429

Available from Amazon.com or your nearest book retailer. Or, order direct at www.CrystalDreamsPublishing.com.

Return to the Shadows
By Henry Pavlak

Brian Jeffries, an ex-army sniper, returns to New York from two tours of duty in Iraq, planning to attend college to become an architect. After all the death and destruction he had seen, Brian now wants to create and build instead of tear down and destroy. At twenty-one, he fully understands the realities of war and the fragility of life.

The problem is that wherever Brian goes, violence seems to follow.

He lands a part time job as a bouncer to pick up some extra money. On his third night on the job, he hears a commotion in the alley behind the bar where he witnesses a mob murder. Unable to turn a blind eye to violence, Brian gets involved in trying to bring the murderer to justice. Along the way, he comes to the realization that he does not like what he has become, but he finally accepts his role in life and returns to the shadows.

ISBN-13:9781591462330

Available from Amazon.com or your nearest book retailer. Or, order direct at www.CrystalDreamsPublishing.com.

Serial Terror
By Mark De Binder

Chase Benton founded his private organization to do what the FBI and other law enforcement agencies can't: quickly catch and destroy the most evil and cunning criminals in the country. His top team of psychics, special agents and a state-of-the-art supercomputer guarantee success.

In this series debut, Chase squares off against an enemy from his past who will stop at nothing to destroy him and his foundation. Working in parallel with other law enforcement agencies, Chase and team confront three of the FBI's most wanted serial killers. As they race to stop the gruesome murders and wholesale slaughter, their efforts are thwarted by Chase's nemesis and the FBI's own Profiling Group.

To overcome these opposing forces, Chase and his team are forced to tap into their psychic connections and CLAIR, the artificial intelligence supercomputer, to out maneuver his opponents. From New Hampshire to Maryland to Washington and Maine, the forces battle one another in a gripping, non-stop page turner.

ISBN-13:9781591463924

Available from Amazon.com or your nearest book retailer. Or, order direct at www.CrystalDreamsPublishing.com.

Identity Theft - It's Murder!
By Connie Slocum

Patricia Farmer headed off to college with a car full of friends and a trunk full of dreams. Like all freshman, she was just beginning to learn who she was. Unaware of the forks in the road of life that lurked just ahead, she had no idea that her forks would have more than the usual set of prongs. There was studying, forensic lab, friends and the normal chaos of college life.

Plus, she had two very different men in her life. Scott was as clean cut as they came, and Todd, his complete opposite, the mysterious bad boy. Todd was the type females can't keep away from, the one she thought her friend Tina was in love with. Her attraction to both of them was overwhelming. Still, she juggled it all without faltering until her best friend Sunny was arrested for murder.

She vows to clear her friend's name. The problem escalates when she has to be on all of the roads at once, crossing paths with a serial killer. But which fork is the right one? And who is the murderer?

Find out by reading this new novel by author Connie Slocum: Identity Theft - It's Murder!

ISBN-13:9781591463771

Available from Amazon.com or your nearest book retailer. Or, order direct at www.CrystalDreamsPublishing.com.

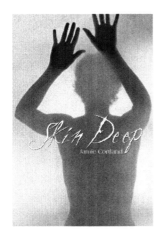

Skin Deep

By Jamie Cortland

Chase Benton founded his private
He's looking for you . . . On
the beaches; the tennis courts;
in cocktail lounges, up-scale
restaurants and coffee houses. When
you meet him, he will be charming,
engaging and compelling . . . all but
impossible to resist. Others will feel
his menacing aura, but you will not.
And so it was for Evelyn who was
still half-way in love with her super-star ex-husband. Once
caught in his web, she discovered he was not the man of
her dreams. Dropping his mask, he became the hideous
creature of her nightmares. Her only thought was to find a
way to escape.

ISBN-13:9781591460978

Reunion With a Killer

By Rod Summitt and Richard Edgerton

Lee Bishop, a hardware sales rep, decides to make his last cross-country sales trip by car instead of flying. One of his main reasons was to stop in the town in Iowa where he went to school, both to see the school again and to visit with his old college roommate who is now the president of the local bank with whom Lee has been corresponding through yearly Christmas cards.

When he arrives in town, he tries to hook up with his old friend, Carl Kyle, but is told by his friend that he must leave town on business and that they won't be able to meet. Lee decides to drop in at the bank anyway for a quick hello, and when directed to Kyle's office sees a man who is a complete stranger.

Lee learns that while the man at the bank is obviously not his old friend, he is accepted by the townsfolk as the man who was once Lee's roommate at the local college. About ready to continue his trip and leave the perplexing puzzle behind him, Lee discovers that the editor of the local newspaper is Pete Riley, another old friend from college and enlists his help in solving the mystery of just who is the bank president and what has happened to Carl Kyle.

ISBN-13:9781591460985

CPSIA information can be obtained at www.ICGtesting.com
Printed in the USA
LVOW091256291011

252571LV00003B/18/P